'Could you an   the way we we

Jack continued, 'Could we start all over again?' Before Kate could even react, his mouth was on hers, gently seeking an answer.

She felt weak and dizzy, helpless to control her arms as they wound themselves around his neck. She'd only ever felt like this once before...and only ever with him.

'You still feel it, don't you, Kate? There is still hope for us...if we can only let go of the past.'

'Oh, Jack...' She let her hands slide from his shoulders, shaking her head. 'I shouldn't have let you kiss me, Jack.' She looked up at him with stricken eyes. 'Jack, I'm getting married in two weeks!'

Elizabeth Duke was born in Adelaide, South Australia, but has lived in Melbourne all her married life. She trained as a librarian and has worked in many different types of libraries, but she was always secretly writing. Her first published book was a children's novel, after which she successfully tried her hand at romance writing. She has since given up her work as a librarian to write romance full-time. When she isn't writing or reading, she loves to travel with her husband John, either within Australia or overseas, gathering inspiration and background material for future romances. She and John have a married son and daughter, who now have children of their own.

Recent titles by the same author:

THE HUSBAND DILEMMA

BY
ELIZABETH DUKE

MILLS & BOON®

All the characters in this book have no existence outside the imagination of the author, and have no relation whatsoever to anyone bearing the same name or names. They are not even distantly inspired by any individual known or unknown to the author, and all the incidents are pure invention.

First published in Great Britain 1998
Harlequin Mills & Boon Limited,
Eton House, 18-24 Paradise Road, Richmond, Surrey TW9 1SR

© Elizabeth Duke 1998

ISBN 0 263 81462 9

Set in Times Roman 10 ½ on 12 pt.
02-9902-50405 C1

Printed and bound in Norway
by AIT Trondheim AS, Trondheim

CHAPTER ONE

KATE stared at her reflection in the mirrored wall of
Madame Yvette's Exclusive Bridal Fashions. The slender golden-haired woman in the classic white wedding
gown stared back.

She felt a quiver of panic.

The wedding was so close. Less than three weeks
away. Three short weeks.

It hit her for the first time. In just three weeks she
would be a married woman, a wife, a life partner. Paired
for ever with one man.

This was the biggest step she would ever take in her
life. The most important, most life-changing, most permanent step…if you believed that marriage was for life,
which she did. It was a bit scary.

Not that she had any doubts. She straightened her
shoulders. Brendan loved her and she loved him. Even
more important, she liked and trusted him. He might not
be the most exciting man in the world, the most passionate man in the world. He might not have stunning
good looks or a tanned athlete's physique. He might not
send her blood roaring through her veins the way…the
way…

She had a fleeting image of piercing blue eyes, wind-
swept black hair and powerful sun-bronzed shoulders.

She blinked the disturbingly vivid image away. The
last man in the world she wanted to think about—now
or ever—was Jonathan Savage. The way he could still

5

haunt her on occasion, could still slip into her dreams at night, was maddening. It made no sense. It was nearly five years since that tumultuous day on Shelly Beach...the promising dream that had turned to a nightmare.

She hadn't seen or heard of him since...or wanted to. Not consciously, at any rate.

Of course, it was the image of her gallant rescuer *Jack*, not the despised Jonathan Savage, that occasionally haunted her dreams. And Jack didn't exist. He'd been a fantasy figure, a dream man, and dream men were illusions. She'd spent years looking...hoping...for another man who could make her feel the way Jack had— *Jack*, not Jonathan Savage—but no other man ever had. She'd finally realised that she was chasing after a phantom, an impossible dream, and had come back to cold reality.

Passion...feelings...weren't to be trusted. It was trust, reliability, steadiness in a man that mattered, not how a man made you feel. Fire and passion only clouded the issue, blinding you to the harshly real human failings underneath...like heartless indifference and ruthless insensitivity!

She lifted her chin, relegating Jonathan Savage back to where he belonged...in the past. It was just pre-wedding jitters. All brides suffered them at some time or other. She'd panicked for a second, seeing herself dressed as a bride, realising how close the wedding was, how final it was. She was being silly. Everything was just fine. Everything was *going* to be fine.

'You're going to make a beautiful bride, Kate,' a soft voice said from behind.

She turned her head, and summoned a quick smile.

Melanie, her bridesmaid and best friend from their school days, as well as her current flatmate, had come to watch her final fitting. Only the hem and some beading needed to be done now...and Madame Yvette, kneeling on the floor, was busily working on the hem right at this moment.

'And you're going to be a beautiful bridesmaid, Mel,' Kate said warmly. 'You'll look stunning in that crimson dress we've chosen, with your dark hair.'

'Always the bridesmaid, never the bride...' Melanie's smile was rueful. 'This will be my third time. Not that I'm not delighted to be your bridesmaid, Kate, you mustn't think—'

'Your turn will come, Mel. It's amazing no one's snapped you up already. You have the loveliest face in the world, you don't have an ounce of malice in you, and you'll make some lucky guy the most wonderful wife...and be a perfect mother too. You've even had practice looking after babies and young children, with your work at the crèche.'

'I think men find me boring,' Melanie said with a sigh. She was a real homebody, happier spending her time curled up on a sofa reading a book or making dolls and toys for local fêtes and hospitals—or for her young charges at the crèche—than playing sport or going to parties. And yet she was far from dull. They often saw movies or plays together—when Kate's schedule permitted—and a lively discussion always followed. Mel was a delight to be with.

'But never mind about me. What about *you*, Kate?' Melanie probed gently. 'You were looking a bit wistful a moment ago. You're not getting cold feet?' she asked half-jokingly. But her soft dark eyes were concerned. 'You…do love Brendan, don't you?'

Kate gulped and turned back to the mirror. Melanie knew nothing about her brief, painful encounter with Jonathan Savage five years ago. There was only one other person who did know, and Diana was working in New York these days. Even before she'd left Australia, not long after their disastrous trip to Shelly Beach together, Diana had kept quiet about it, aware of Kate's sensitivity on the subject.

Kate herself had never breathed a word to a living soul about what had happened on Queensland's Sunshine Coast on that unseasonably hot September day. It was far too humiliating.

'Of course I love Brendan.' She injected surprise into her voice at the question. 'He's an easy guy to love.' A thoroughly nice, thoroughly safe, thoroughly dependable guy. Not a heartless, high-flying, sweep-you-off-your-feet powerhouse like Jonathan Savage. Brendan was a gentle, steady, reliable, *average* sort of guy—average height, average looks, average temperament—with a better than average job as a tax accountant, running his own successful business.

There had been nothing average about Jack. *Jonathan Savage*, she corrected, with a hardening of her mouth.

Nothing steady or reliable either.

Poor Charlotte… Kate's eyes misted as she thought of her sister.

'There!' Madame Yvette rose to her feet. 'All finished. The gown will be ready for you to pick up by the end of next week, dear. Let me help you out of it now…'

Kate glanced at her watch as the beautiful silk and

lace wedding gown was removed and whisked away. 'Oh, heck, Mel, I'll have to fly. I'm on duty at three!'

It was nearly that already.

'You go ahead.' Melanie waved her away. 'I have to buy my mother a birthday present, to take home at the weekend.' It was her afternoon off from the crèche.

Kate nodded, thanked her for coming, then dashed out to where she'd parked her car, uttering a string of curses when she found a parking ticket on the windscreen.

Her parking meter had expired! Furious with herself for not sending Melanie out during her fitting to feed in extra coins, she flounced into the driver's seat and sped off in the direction of the hospital. She knew she could well end up with a speeding ticket as well, but better that than being late. She prided herself on her punctuality.

The doctors' car park looked aggravatingly crammed with cars as she bowled through the self-opening gates. Lowly residents didn't have reserved spaces. She would just have to drive up and down the rows of cars until she found a vacant spot.

Her eyes lit up as she spied a clear space. She swung the car into the vacant bay with a sigh of relief—only to groan in frustration when she saw the sign in front of her. *'Nursing Director Only.'* Damn! She'd wasted precious seconds. She backed out again far too fast...and heard the sickening crunch of metal on metal.

'Oh, no!' she moaned, slamming her foot on the brake. She hadn't seen the car passing behind her, and the driver, naturally, wouldn't have been expecting her to back out a mere second after she'd nosed her way in! 'Damn, damn, *damn*!' she fumed. She had no one to blame but herself!

She jumped out of the car, hoping the other driver would be someone she knew so they could settle any damage details later. Hoping that the damage, if any, was minimal.

The driver of the other car—an expensive-looking BMW, she noted in dismay—was already stepping out of the driver's seat, unfolding his considerable frame.

Just her luck to strike a big gun, she thought with a sinking heart. He was obviously a visiting consultant or professor, not a mere resident like herself. Worse, he was a doctor she didn't know. A man of imposing presence, with the height and build of a gladiator—a sophisticated gladiator in a charcoal-grey suit.

'What the hell were you thinking of, backing out like that?' he roared, bending down to examine a large dent in the side of his car. 'Look what you've done! This is a brand-new car!'

'I'm sorry,' Kate mumbled. Anyone would think she'd done it on purpose! A snap glance revealed that her own car had suffered no damage at all—thanks to the solid rear bumper bar. 'I—I noticed that I'd swung into a reserved space, and I was just...' She trailed off as he straightened and they came face to face for the first time.

A devastating swooshing sensation swept through her, as if all her blood and everything else inside her were rushing from her body. As if she were dissolving. Liquefying. The car park spun. Her head spun.

It couldn't be.

She stared, trying madly to pull herself together, trying madly to stay upright.

It was *Jack*!

No, not Jack... Icy reality clawed its way back, swamping that initial, distressingly emotional reaction.

'Jonathan Savage,' she hissed through her teeth.

A very different Jonathan Savage from the bronzed, half-naked Samson who'd plucked her from the sea five years ago...

CHAPTER TWO

'KATE, don't waste this glorious sunshine. You go ahead down to the beach,' Diana urged. 'I'll join you after the police have been. They said not to touch anything, so there's nothing you can do here, and they won't want us both underfoot.'

'Are you sure?' Kate glanced over the chaos around them.

'Quite sure. I feel bad enough as it is, bringing you all the way up here to Queensland for nothing. I thought Charlotte's briefcase would have been safe here at my beach-house, locked away in a cupboard.'

Kate and her sister's friend Diana—a high-powered merchant banker just back from a two-year assignment in London—had arrived at Shelly Beach less than an hour ago to find that burglars had robbed Diana's beach-house in her absence. Everything of any value had gone. The TV set, the video, the microwave, the radio.

And Charlotte's briefcase. The briefcase Kate's sister had entrusted to Diana's care two years ago, shortly before her shock suicide. It was the reason Diana had brought Kate up here—so she could hand it over to Kate in private.

The briefcase contained highly delicate papers, Charlotte had confided to Diana. Papers she wasn't ready to deal with yet and didn't want to leave lying around at the family home for her father to find, or at the hospital where she'd worked.

'Could you look after it for me for a while?' she'd begged Diana. 'If I'm hit by a bus or anything,' she'd added—jokingly, Diana had thought, 'you can hand it over to Kate. She can decide what to do with it. But not for a year or so, OK? Let the dust settle.'

And now the briefcase was gone, along with whatever personal papers Charlotte had locked away inside. For Diana's sake, Kate hadn't shown how dismayed she was that the last clue to her sister's tragic suicide had gone.

Not that we need any more clues, she reflected darkly. Jonathan Savage is to blame for my sister's death. If he hadn't walked out on Charlotte...if he hadn't been so cruel and uncaring...

Her eyes hardened as she thought of the note Charlotte had scribbled before drifting into that last deadly sleep: *'I can't live with the pain. Johnnie, forgive me.'*

The pain of losing him...

Charlotte—hard-nosed, self-centred, blazingly ambitious Charlotte, who'd never been seriously interested in any man before, let alone head-over-heels in love—had been crazy about Jonathan Savage. They'd worked at the same hospital...trained together...spent most of their spare time together. And then he'd walked out on her, just like that, flying off to America without a backward glance.

It had devastated Charlotte. In her despair, she'd messed up a vital interview a week later, losing the surgical registrar position she'd craved for so long and worked so hard for.

For Charlotte, that must have been the last straw. Three weeks later she'd swallowed a bottle full of lethal pills. And even then she'd been thinking of *him*. 'For-

give me,' she'd written…as if she'd been freeing him of any blame or possible self-recrimination.

But Kate and her family *did* blame him. Jonathan Savage, the callous monster, had a lot to answer for. Kate drew in her lips, wondering if he had any idea how much pain and suffering he'd left behind. It was just as well he'd left Australia, or *he'd* have been suffering too, if her family had anything to do with it.

'Off you *go*, Kate.' Diana bundled her out through the door. 'Better not go swimming, though…at least not on your own,' she advised. 'The beach isn't patrolled and there's quite an undertow. Not that it stops the surfies…or even swimmers on a calm day.'

Kate gave in, pausing only to change into a one-piece swimsuit, pulling a loose shirt over the top before grabbing her beachbag and towel, and the sketchbook she never went anywhere without. The realisation that Charlotte's secrets were now lost—probably for ever—had cast a pall over her. Hopefully, the Queensland sun and the fresh sea air would brighten her up a bit.

A faint melancholy still clung to her as she crossed the low grassy sand dunes to the beach, though the fresh salty tang drifting up from the sea and the seeping warmth of the brilliant September sun did much to restore her spirits.

She came to a halt where the sandhills sloped down to the wide expanse of pure white sand, her gaze doing a lazy sweep of the beach. It was almost deserted…except for one lone male running along the shoreline.

She found her eyes following him…not warily, as might have been wise, but in sheer admiration. He looked like an Olympic athlete…a magnificent specimen, all rippling muscle, well-honed sinew, and smooth golden flesh that gleamed like burnished mahogany in the bright Queensland sunlight. For a startled second she thought he was stark naked, until she realised he was wearing brief swim-trunks that matched the colour of his tan.

Still watching him, she began to descend the sandy slope leading down to the beach, her feet leaving deep imprints in the soft grainy sand. As if sensing her presence, the bronzed Adonis glanced up and saw her. He waved as he loped along. She began to raise her own hand, then thought better of it and let it drop. He was a complete stranger to her, and there was nobody else around. Best not to encourage him...though it was tempting.

He kept on jogging at the same easy pace, away from her now, and she relaxed—noting at the same time that his magnificent physique was equally as stunning from behind, his massive shoulders tapering to lean hips, his powerful legs as fluid in motion as a loping jungle cat.

Her eyes followed him as the distance between them grew...and grew...until he was just a hazy outline against the pearly wash of the sunlit beach.

She found a snug little hollow at the base of the sand-hills and spread out her towel on the sand. Glancing round to make sure she was still alone, she stripped off the long loose shirt covering her swimsuit—a low-backed, high-legged creation in a riot of different colours—and settled down on her towel to sunbake.

But after a few minutes she sat up again, and on an impulse reached for the sketchbook and pencil she'd brought down to the beach with her, just in case.

Just in case she saw something that inspired her.

A wicked smile curved her lips. Inspired her? That was putting it mildly!

She sketched a quick pencil outline, from memory, of the magnificently built hunk she'd seen—first a side profile, then from behind, showing his body in motion, his hand raised in a wave. His face, half turned towards her, was indistinct, due to the distance between them, so all she could give was an impression of a strong square jaw, dark eyes under heavy brows, and thick black hair, cut reasonably short...but every other detail of his impressive frame was clearly etched in her memory.

She became so absorbed in her task that she didn't realise for a while how hot the afternoon had become, or how fiercely the sun's rays were penetrating her lightly oiled skin, until she'd finished her sketches to her satisfaction and tossed the sketchbook down.

'Whew! It's *hot*!' She sat for a moment, gazing longingly at the waves breaking on the shore and the glittering blue water beyond. She remembered Diana's warning about not going swimming alone, but the water looked so inviting. And so safe.

There wasn't a heavy surf today, which probably accounted for the absence of any surfies in the water. There were no swimmers either, but it was midweek and school term-time, and this was a secluded beach considered dangerous for swimming, as a sign above the beach warned.

There did appear to be a strong undertow sucking the swirling water back from the shoreline, but Kate was confident she could deal with it, if she didn't go out too far. She'd always been a strong swimmer—a swimming champion, in fact, during her schooldays—which had toned and strengthened her body, despite its slender build.

So why not? Just a quick dip, to cool herself down. She'd go out no further than waist height. She needed something to relax her and cool her down after coming all the way up here during uni term to find that her reason for coming had vanished.

Having made up her mind, she jumped up and headed for the water, pausing as she reached the shoreline to glance around. There was still no one else on the beach, or anywhere in sight, and the spectacularly built jogger had disappeared, perhaps taking a shortcut across the sandhills above the beach, back to wherever he'd come from.

As a gently rolling wave crashed onto the shore and broke, she dipped her toe into the fizzing white foam swirling across the sand towards her. It felt good. Really good.

She took a step forward, and then another, picking her way through the bubbly shallows, resisting the pull of the undertow as the water surged back from the shore. She waded through the tumbling froth to waist height, then began to paddle gently, following the swell of the waves as they came, relishing the sensual coolness of the water as it flowed over her skin and streamed through her hair.

It was pure bliss...until it gradually dawned on her that she could no longer touch the bottom. As she tried to head back to shore, she realised she was making no headway, that some force was exerting pressure against her, dragging at her arms, her body, her legs.

Alarm snapped her out of her euphoria as she realised she was caught in a strong rip. She could no longer see the beach for the swell of the waves. All she could see was blue water and clear sky, the waves forcing her to struggle even harder. An icy fear gripped her.

I'm not going to make it, she thought in sudden panic, and had an agonising glimpse of her father's face, and her mother's, at the loss of another daughter. She couldn't let it happen! She began to fight with all her might against the dragging current, kicking with her legs and thrashing her arms in a desperate attempt to force her way back to shore.

But she knew it was no good. She was making no headway at all, and she was tiring. Fast.

Her flailing hands connected with something solid. She screamed and lashed out wildly, thinking it must be a shark.

As she blindly struck out, squeezing her eyes shut against her turbulent splashes, she felt a hard knock to her upper cheek, then heard a man's voice rasping, 'Don't fight me, I'll help you!' as strong hands grasped her by the shoulders and swung her round.

An iron-muscled arm clamped around her from behind, across her heaving breasts, crushing her against what felt like an equally hard male body...an amazingly powerful body with massive strength, massive muscles, massive control. Even in her terror, she felt strangely safe in his arms...protected...as if she could indeed rely on this man to help her. As if she could place her life in his hands.

She went limp in his arms.

'Good. Now...gently kick your legs,' grated her rescuer as he struck out with his free arm, his other holding her in that vice-like grip. 'We'll make it if we pull together...if you don't panic! If you're too tired to kick, just relax and let me do the work.'

She didn't panic. Or relax. She used her arms and legs to help as much as she could, though she had a sneaky feeling he didn't really need her feeble attempts at assistance; he just hadn't wanted her to fight him or try to hold him back.

Instead of fighting against the rip, he struck out diagonally across it, gradually making headway until suddenly the undercurrent dragging at them wasn't there any more, and Kate realised with a gasp of relief that they'd managed to free themselves from its insidious pull. They were going to make it.

As if she'd ever had any doubt, from the moment her Herculean rescuer had seized her in his capable arms. Mighty arms...mighty shoulders...mighty legs. He had to be the powerful runner she'd seen on the beach earlier...he couldn't be anyone else. How lucky that he'd seen her!

Now that they'd freed themselves from the pull of the undertow, the rest was easy. They even managed to catch a rolling wave, which swept them both in without either needing to make any effort at all. The wave shattered, dumping them on the shore in a tumble of white froth and a tangle of arms and legs.

As the water surged back, threatening to drag them back with it, he pulled her out of its sucking reach, onto dry sand. For a moment they both lay gasping, lungs heaving, throats rasping. She was still tangled in his arms, she realised dazedly. Still safe and protected in those great muscled arms.

'Well, my golden mermaid,' he heaved out between ragged breaths, 'we made it.'

She looked up at him through tangled honey-gold curls. Straight into a pair of startlingly blue eyes. Blue! She'd imagined they would be black...or a deep brown. It must have been his thick black lashes and heavy dark brows that, from a distance, had given the impression of darkness.

'You s-saved my life,' she whispered in wonder. And realised her teeth were chattering. With reaction rather than cold. The arms round her were warm, keeping *her* warm. 'Th-thank you.'

She expected him to berate her for her stupidity in going swimming on her own, but he didn't. Maybe he was afraid she'd dissolve into floods of hysterical tears if he started chastising her.

'You're all right?' He stroked clinging tendrils of damp hair back from her face.

'I'm fine...thanks to you,' she answered breathily. He had a strong face to match the rest of him, she noted, absorbing each detail with an artist's eye. *Or a woman's?* A well-defined jawline, a straight nose, firm lips...an arresting rather than classically handsome face. It was his eyes that made it remarkable. Even in her shaky state, her fingers itched to sketch him, to clarify the blurred impression she'd made before.

'You're going to have a black eye, I'm afraid.' His fingers lightly traced the fine skin above her left cheek. 'Sorry...it was an accident. Your face connected with my elbow when you were fighting me off.'

'I—I thought you were a shark,' she admitted sheepishly. 'I didn't think there was anyone else around.' She gulped in a couple of deep breaths. 'Where did you spring from?'

'I decided to come back to the beach for another run.'

There was a distinct glitter in the blue eyes now that caused her to wonder, with a sudden warmth to her cheeks, if he'd come back not for a run, but to take another look at the lone female on the beach? Any man with a physique like his, with stunning eyes like his, must know he had a first-rate chance with any girl he set his cap at. She felt an odd little quiver at the thought, and quickly dismissed it as derision rather than jealousy.

'I saw you in the water from the sandhills,' he told her, 'and decided I'd better follow you…knowing the currents along here can get a bit tricky at times, if you go out too far.'

'But I didn't—' She stopped. 'I mean I didn't real-ise…' She began to tremble. She hadn't realised a lot of things, it occurred to her now. The danger from the sea. The danger from this stranger holding her. Not dan-ger to her physically. Danger to her emotions. To her peace of mind.

To her heart.

'Obviously not,' came his dry comment. He slid his great arm out from beneath her. 'You're shivering. I'll get your towel.'

'There's no n—' But as she tried to get up her legs buckled beneath her. They felt like tingly, useless rubber.

'Here…I'll carry you.' Before she could protest, he swept her up in his powerful arms as if she were no heavier than a child. Or a bubble of froth. 'Better still…I'll take you back to wherever you're staying. Where I'll know you'll be safe.'

Her eyes snapped wide. 'No!' She didn't want Diana knowing she'd gone in swimming alone, despite her warnings, and had almost drowned. 'Just—just dump me where I left my towel. I'll be fine.'

'I'm not leaving you alone.' His tone said he meant it. 'You might get into more strife.'

She thought of arguing—did he think she might actually go back into the water again if he left her alone?—but she decided against it, his vow not to leave her alone causing a shiver of excitement all the way down to her toes. She didn't *want* him to leave her, she realised. She wanted him to stay here with her...wanted to get to know him better...wanted to know all about him. She owed him her life. Already she felt curiously close to him...drawn to him...mysteriously connected in some strange cosmic way.

Simply because he'd saved her life?

Or because he was the most exciting, most dynamic, most incredible-looking man she'd ever met?

He lowered her onto the striped beach-towel she'd left spread out on the sand. Then he scooped up her discarded shirt and draped it round her shoulders, before dropping down beside her.

She was suddenly very conscious of his near-nakedness, gulping at the huge expanse of bronzed well-muscled chest so close to her, the enormous shoulders, the powerful thighs, the fine dark hairs that went all the way down to—

She flicked her gaze away.

'You're sure you're all right?' He had the deepest voice, with a richness that rumbled right through her.

She nodded, unconsciously flicking her tongue over her lips. 'Are—are *you* all right?' she asked belatedly. Just because he was built like a rock, it didn't mean he was invincible. She'd thought her sister invincible once.

Tough, self-reliant, hard as nails... But when the man in her life had tossed her aside, she'd disintegrated.

What if her rescuer had a weak heart under all those rippling muscles? Or some other hidden complaint? She would be responsible if...

She shivered.

He seemed surprised at her question, that she would care about *him*. 'Mermaid-hunting appeals to me,' he said lightly, brushing off her concern.

Mermaid-hunting? Or *girl*-hunting? she wondered, squinting up at him. He was still a male. A very sexy male. As virile as he was strong, she had no doubt. With a heart and a constitution to match, most likely. She felt herself blushing like a schoolgirl.

He traced a light finger over her left cheek. For a breathless second she thought he was drawing attention to her blushes, until he commented. 'You have quite a bruise under your eye. And some swelling. You should do something about it.'

She reached up to lightly finger the tender spot—making sure he'd removed his own hand first. She could feel the swelling. The tenderness.

'Damn,' she muttered. Now she certainly couldn't go back...not just yet. The police must be there by now, and if she turned up at the beach-house with a noticeable black eye there could be awkward questions. Her Herculean rescuer might get into trouble for causing the injury...even though he'd struck her accidentally while saving her life. They mightn't believe her...or *him*.

Or she might get into trouble for going swimming at a beach that was unsafe and unpatrolled. She remembered the warning sign above the beach. 'SWIMMING

HERE IS DANGEROUS'. Not 'forbidden', thankfully, but 'dangerous' was bad enough.

'You need some ice on it, quick smart.' He was inspecting it so closely that she felt prickly and breathless. 'Won't you let me take you home?' He touched her arm.

'No…thanks.' It was a husky croak. His touch, which had made her feel so safe and protected earlier, now seemed positively lethal. She looked up at him appealingly. 'I—I can't go back yet…'

He smiled. A faintly teasing, achingly attractive smile. 'Afraid of getting into trouble with your parents, are you, for going swimming on your own and getting into difficulties?'

'I'm not with my parents!' What did he think she was? A rebellious teenager, going swimming behind their backs? She jutted her chin. She might be nineteen—strictly speaking still a teenager—but she was *nearly* twenty, and she'd been living with other uni students for close on two years!

'I'm staying here with a friend,' she told him, her tone crisp. 'She had to call the police because her beach-house has been burgled and she—she wanted me out of the way.' She flushed. 'Look, I know it was stupid, going swimming on my own. I won't do it again,' she promised, in case he thought she might.

'Good.' A satisfied nod. 'So…you don't want to go home just yet?' He quirked a dark eyebrow, the dazzling blue eyes turning her bones to putty.

She shook her head. Not with a great bruised lump under her eye that would be hard to explain away. 'I—I'll wait awhile and hope the swelling goes down.' She swallowed. Hard. Would he decide to stay with her?

'It's more likely to get worse if you don't put some

ice on it. I could provide a cold compress for you if you'd like to pop across to my beach-house. It's just across the sand dunes, overlooking the beach. You can see it from here…through those trees.' He raised a hand and pointed.

Her head snapped back. Go to *his* beach-house? 'Oh, no…I couldn't do that…' Even as she protested, a part of her was urging her to accept…to follow wherever he wanted to take her. But wisely, perhaps, another part of her was more cautious. *Oh, I'll just bet you'd like to take me back to your beach-house…a virile hunk like you. You think I want to risk getting into more trouble?*

Feeling flustered, and oddly frustrated at the same time, she grabbed her beach-bag and fumbled inside. 'I…I'd better go. Maybe if I put sunglasses on I can hide my black eye.' At least until she could get to Diana's bathroom and dab some cover-up on it.

She found them and slipped them on—only to yelp. 'Ouch!' and tug them off again as the frames dug into the tender swelling under her eye. So much for that idea!

He made the decision for her. 'Come on, we're going to my place.' He rose to his feet, brushing the sand off with his hands. She gulped as she felt a strong urge to do it for him. 'You won't have to come inside the house. I'll bring the ice-pack out to you. I've a sports pack in the freezer. I never go anywhere without it.'

'You're a sportsman? An athlete?' Her gaze flickered over the deeply tanned muscles, the powerful legs. It was a delaying tactic. Should she go with him or not? She snatched in a badly needed breath.

He looked down at her, a faint smile on his lips. 'Just an amateur jogger…to keep myself fit. I used to play rugby at university, and now I try to jog or play tennis when I get the chance, so the muscle won't turn to fat.'

She couldn't imagine muscles like his ever turning to fat. Not in a million years. 'When you get the chance?' she echoed. Obviously a busy man. 'You're on holiday at the moment?'

Where had he come from? she wondered, hoping he'd tell her that he'd come up from Sydney. *Please, not Brisbane, or Melbourne, or, heaven forbid, the far west coast.* She crossed her fingers for luck, a habit she'd had since her schooldays. *Please say Sydney.* Was it too much to hope for?

He paused a moment before answering, as if considering whether to reveal any more about himself. 'Not exactly. It was my brother's wedding last weekend...in Brisbane,' he told her. 'I'm taking a few days' break here at Shelly Beach—staying at my brother's beachhouse—before I fly back to America.'

America! Her heart plunged. It wasn't fair... She let her breath out in a sigh. To find a man like this...and then to lose him again so quickly! 'You *live* in America?' She held her breath. He sounded Australian, not American. What was he doing in America? How long was he planning to stay there?

'For the time being I do. I'm doing some specialist training in New York. I plan to come back to Australia eventually. Hopefully to work in Sydney...where I lived before.'

Her eyes lit up, her pulse quickening. 'Really? That's where I live!' She felt herself flushing. How gauche and over-eager he must think her! A man with his looks and experience of the world—he'd be in his late twenties, she hazarded—must be used to older, cooler, more sophisticated women. Women with far more experience and panache than a lowly university student like Kate Warren-Smith.

Not that she *looked* only nineteen. She rallied at the thought. She'd been told often enough that she looked years older. And her unusually low, husky voice often fooled people too. Maybe he hadn't guessed...

'Uh...what line of work are you in?' she asked in a cooler, more off-hand tone. What she really wanted to know was: *How long is your training in America going to take?*

He seemed to hesitate again, and she bit down on her lip. Was she asking too many questions?

'I'm a doctor.'

A *doctor*? So he had a brain as well as a magnificent body and heroic tendencies! 'That's what I'm going to be!' she burst out, forgetting about being cool and sophisticated. Amazingly, they had something in common! She could feel her heart beating wildly under her loose shirt. And he was planning to come back to Australia to practise. To Sydney...her home town!

'I'm doing medicine myself,' she gushed, careful not to mention that she was only in her second year at med school. Near the *end* of her second year, she would tell him, if he asked.

'Are you now?'

The way he said it caused her eyes to waver under his. Was he laughing at her? Mocking her? The narrowed blue eyes were difficult to read. There was no noticeable twinkling or obvious derision that she could tell. If anything, they looked more guarded than amused.

And then she recalled what he'd said a moment ago. *Specialist* training. Her heart dipped. He was a medical high-flier. One of the high-and-mighty élite. A *specialist* doctor. A member of the so-called boys' club.

And she was a mere medical student!

She sighed, her spirits plunging further. Medical specialists—especially surgeons—were notoriously arrogant and ego-driven. They were remote, God-like figures who lived in their own exalted little world, seldom coming down to human level, seldom caring about anything but their own narrow, if vital, field of work.

Look at her father.

Not that all specialist doctors were as emotionally remote as her father. She glanced hopefully up at her husky rescuer. She'd met one or two who had lives and interests outside their own absorbing, highly-specialised field. A few even had a sense of fun, a sense of humour. A *heart*.

But perhaps she was being unfair to her father. He'd shown two years ago, after the death of his favourite daughter—his bright shining hope—that he did have a heart, that he *could* feel. And suffer, just like other mortals.

She thought fleetingly of her mother, his caring, compassionate suburban GP wife, who'd suffered the most over the years from his remoteness and emotional neglect. Even though they'd been living apart at the time Charlotte had died, her mother had immediately rushed to her husband's side, offering comfort and warmth. Edith Warren-Smith had never stopped loving him, despite his emotional neglect, despite the hurt he'd caused her, despite leaving him for eighteen months, taking her younger daughter with her.

Kate wondered if she would have been as forgiving.

'What field are you specialising in?' she asked curiously, suddenly feeling the need to know. Orthopaedic surgery, perhaps? He looked the type. Fit, strong, sporty. A jogger and a tennis player. It meant he must have some sort of life outside medicine.

Her skin prickled as an uneasy memory stirred. He was from Sydney, he'd said...and he was training in America. Training to become a specialist. A specialist *surgeon*? Although she knew that must apply to dozens of Australian doctors, a sudden, frightening suspicion flickered...only to die—mercifully—the moment he answered.

'I'm doing neurosurgery.'

She blinked. He was training to be a *brain* surgeon? Her momentary relief that he wasn't doing cardiac surgery, like her father, turned to dismay. A neurosurgeon was up there with heart surgeons! Maybe even *beyond*. Dammit, why couldn't he have been a plain, simple, ordinary GP like her mother? Like *she* wanted to be herself?

'You won't hold it against me, I hope?' Now he *was* laughing at her. Plainly amused at the shocked look on her face.

She let her eyelashes flutter down, giving a careless laugh of her own. 'Of course not...don't be silly.' Her breast heaved in a quick sigh. Just her luck that the man of her dreams had turned out to be a high-powered specialist surgeon like her father! 'Look...I've wasted enough of your time,' she mumbled. 'I'll be all right, truly. I'll just stay here a while longer. My friend will be here soon. You—you go. And thank you for—'

'You're coming with me.' His tone was as implacable as the set of his jaw. 'Come on.' He reached out a hand to help her up, but she ignored it. 'You can stay out on the lawn, in full view of the other houses. Think you're capable of walking yet? Or do you want me to carry you?'

'I can manage,' she said hastily, giving in far more readily than she would have expected only seconds ago. Her parents, if they only knew, would think she'd gone stark raving mad, agreeing to go off with a perfect stranger. Even if he *was* training to be a brain surgeon!

If he was. Some men would say anything to impress a girl they'd set their sights on. Her mouth twisted in a wry smile. In her case, he couldn't have chosen a worse ploy!

She rose gingerly, testing her legs. They felt more normal now. She pulled her shirt more securely round her shoulders, shook out her towel and thrust it into her beach-bag.

'What's this?' He bent down and picked up her sketchbook.

'I'll take it!' She almost snatched it from him. If he saw she'd been sketching *him*... 'It's just a—just a pad I scribble in.'

'Scribble? You're a writer as well as a medical student?'

She gave a shaky laugh, wishing he wasn't showing such an interest in it. 'I'm not a writer...I just draw a bit—for fun. For myself,' she added quickly, making it plain that her scribbles were for her own eyes only. She tucked the sketchbook firmly under her arm, slung her beach-bag over her shoulder, and looked up at him expectantly.

'Which is the quickest way?' She was anxious to get going, now that the decision had been made. She wanted to put something cold on her swollen eye, and to keep it there long enough for it to have some effect before she sallied off to face Diana. Or the police.

She had no idea how long the ice would take to work its magic. But the prospect of spending some more time in her husky rescuer's company—neurosurgeon or not—was distinctly appealing, sending excited ripples down her spine.

'Let's go up the way you came down. It'll be easier,' he said. Easier for *her* he meant. The slope was gentler there. Nothing, she thought, sliding a surreptitious glance down the length of his impressive frame, would be too difficult for him. A few strides of those great legs would take him anywhere...up any hill...over any obstacle.

He hovered protectively behind her as she made her way across the soft sand, staying close at her heels as she began to climb the sandy slope to the low sandhills behind.

'Am I going to be allowed to know your name?' he asked in his deep warm voice.

She chewed her lip. If she told him her name was Kate Warren-Smith, he'd be bound to ask if she was related to Chester Warren-Smith, the famous heart surgeon. As an Australian, and an ambitious surgeon himself, he must have heard of him. He might even have heard about the Warren-Smiths' brilliant surgeon daughter, who'd died tragically of an overdose. Kate didn't want to face disturbing questions about Charlotte. Even his sympathy would put a dampener on the day.

'First names will do.' He still sounded amused. As if, she thought peevishly, she were a cautious little *ingénue* in his eyes, who'd been told never to talk to strangers, let alone divulge her name or address. She gritted her teeth. So much for appearing older than her years!

• Still…first names sounded safe enough. And at least it would be better than having him call her 'love' or 'honey'.

'My name's Kate,' she tossed over her shoulder, giving him the name she favoured over her full name Catherine. Or Cathy, as Charlotte had called her…even though she'd told her sister repeatedly that she preferred Kate.

'Kate…mmm.' His voice drifted musingly after her. 'It suits you. Far more than Miranda.'

'Miranda?' She turned with faint frown. 'Did you think—?'

'Aren't mermaids usually called Miranda?'

'Oh.' She laughed. And after a second's hesitation asked, 'What's yours?' wondering if she really wanted to know. Any man with the looks and amazing physique—to say nothing of the brilliant future—that this man possessed was bound to have a steady girlfriend already…if not a wife. Though surely if he had a wife she'd be here with him. Maybe she *was* here…sheltering from the heat inside his beach-house. Her spirits took a nosedive at the thought.

'Call me Jack,' he invited from behind.

She half turned, trying to hide a faint yearning in her eyes. Even if he was unattached, it didn't mean he wanted a fling with *her*, or was even attracted to her. He was probably just being kind…taking pity on her because she'd come close to drowning. Or because he felt bad about giving her a black eye.

They made their way across the low sand dunes to the row of beach-houses behind, each one partially screened by trees and scrubby bush. He led her through a clump of overhanging casuarinas to a narrow strip of lawn and a modest house on stilts. A small red car stood under an open carport to one side.

'Here we are, Kate.' He waved to a yellow banana lounger under a cluster of shady palm trees. 'Take a seat here in the shade while I fetch that cold pack. Won't be long.'

He bounded up an outdoor flight of stairs, three at a time. Her eyes followed him, drinking in the power and the lithe grace of his superb body. Again she wondered if he was staying alone in the house, or with a friend or a relative. Or a wife.

The thought that he was more likely to be here alone caused her heart to pick up a beat.

CHAPTER THREE

WHEN he came back, he'd pulled on a white T-shirt. While it hid the deeply tanned flesh of his upper torso, it only accentuated the powerful muscles of his arms and chest and the amazing breadth of his shoulders.

She kept her eyes averted from the skintight swim-trunks below the T-shirt, and the strong tanned legs below that, fixing her gaze to the blue plastic ice-pack in his hand.

'Lie back,' he commanded, dropping to his knees beside the lounger. 'I'm not going to hurt you,' he murmured as her eyes flickered warily. 'I'll just hold the ice-pack in place.'

She did as she was told and lay back. And a moment later, as he carefully administered to her, she found herself wondering all over again how a man so big and strong could have such an amazingly gentle, tender touch, his fingertips barely brushing her skin as he carefully laid the cold compress on the tender swelling below her left eye.

She closed her eyes and kept still, enjoying the soothing coolness as it seeped into her bruised flesh... relishing at the same time the tenderness of those feather-like fingers...the delicious sense of being nurtured...cared for. She knew a few sexy males at uni, but none of them had Jack's sensitivity...or his strength. Or his looks either, for that matter.

Without opening her eyes she asked ingenuously, 'I'm

not holding you up, am I, Jack? Won't your friends or your—er—family be arriving back soon? Or are they already in the house?'

'No need to worry about me.' There was a thread of amusement in his voice, as if he knew what she was really asking. 'I'm here on my own. I don't have any close friends in Queensland, and my brother's my only relative here in Australia.'

On his own...

Her heartbeat went suddenly haywire. Not with apprehension or fear, but with excitement...anticipation...a wild flutter of joy. Anything could happen in a couple of days!

Of course, even longer would be better...if he could stretch his visit to include Sydney.

'Keep still,' Jack rapped. 'You're dislodging the ice-pack.'

'Sorry.' She obediently settled back, her eyes still closed. 'You—er—you're not flying down to Sydney, Jack, to catch up with your friends there?'

She found she was crossing her fingers again, hoping—ridiculously—that he might change his mind and fly down to Sydney in two days' time, perhaps even catching the same plane as Diana and herself, to spend a few days with a *new* friend, before flying back to America. She trembled at the thought.

'You're getting cold,' Jack said, feeling the tremor run through her. 'Or did I hurt you?'

She let one eye flicker open. He hadn't answered her question, she noticed. Obviously he had no thought of flying down to Sydney. He preferred to spend his few spare days here, relaxing on the Sunshine Coast.

'No...I'm fine.' She gulped. His face was very

close…disturbingly close. She could see every line and pore and vein in his deeply tanned face…every separate eyelash fringing the piercing blue eyes…the sooty shadow of regrowth on his chin and jaw. Another tremor shook her.

'You *are* cold.' With his free hand, he began to massage her bare legs. Under the soothing stroke of his palm, her skin felt suddenly burning hot, anything but chilled. 'Not that you feel cold,' he murmured. 'Your skin's as warm as…a new-laid egg. And as smooth. Silky-smooth. Not a single goosebump.'

Her breath seized in her throat, the provocative words affecting her as much as his gently stroking touch. If he wanted to stop her trembling, he was going about it in quite the wrong way!

'It's just the chill from the ice!' she croaked, not wanting him to think she was trembling because of *him*. Even if she was.

'Is it too cold?' he asked, adjusting the pack slightly. 'How's that? Or do you feel you've had enough?'

'No! I mean…I think I could take a bit more,' she assured him breathlessly. 'I'm sure it's helping.' She wanted to keep him close for a bit longer, wanted him to go on stroking her legs, wanted him to go on talking to her in that tantalisingly intimate way.

Wanted him to want *her* as much as she was beginning to want him.

Flustered by the startling thought, by the erotic images swirling through her mind, she blurted out another question. 'How long will it be, Jack, before you come back to Australia?'

His eyes swam over hers, and she had a sensation of

drowning—pleasantly this time, not with fear in her heart, as she'd felt earlier in that treacherous rip.

'Maybe sooner than I thought,' he said softly, only to draw back, as if he'd startled himself by the admission.

'Tell me, Kate,' he added in a lighter vein, making her wonder if he'd changed the subject deliberately, 'have you always wanted to be a doctor?'

Her breath whispered out in a faint sigh. She would far rather have heard *why* he was thinking of coming home sooner than planned. 'No...not always,' she admitted. 'I once dreamed of being an artist,' she told him honestly, giving a brief laugh as she said it, to show him the dream was well and truly behind her.

'An artist?' His gaze veered towards the sketchbook she'd dropped on the grass beside her beach-bag. 'What kind of artist?' he asked curiously. 'Landscapes? Modern art? Still life?'

'Portraits.' She felt herself blushing under the cold pack, and hoping fervently that he wouldn't take it into his head to snatch up her sketchbook and peek inside. But he would never do that. Not without her permission...

Would he?

'So...it's faces and figures that interest you.'

Figures... The heat in her cheeks intensified.

'I...it was just a childish pipe dream,' she told him, dismissing the once burning passion. 'I used to draw a lot when I was younger. I loved it. But in my final year at school I...decided to do medicine instead. Art's just a hobby now,' she said with a shrug.

She blinked away a sudden image of her sister...the sister who'd been so determined to follow in their famous father's footsteps. Charlotte's death had changed everything. Taking up medicine, as her sister had, had seemed the best way to ease her parents' pain...to make them proud of her, as they'd been of Charlotte. She'd hoped to make up in some small way for their tragic loss.

But she was going to be a decidedly pale shadow of her sister, she was sadly aware, because she intended to be a simple, ordinary GP, like her mother, not a prestigious heart surgeon like her father...like Charlotte had hoped to be. Her father, she knew, still had hopes that she would specialise, but her mind was made up. She wanted to be a more down-to-earth, patient-oriented doctor, like her mother—dealing with the whole of a person, mind, body and soul, not just focusing on one small, if vital part.

'So you chose to do medicine...just like that.' The piercing blue eyes glimmered under her gaze. She wasn't sure if it was in admiration...or amusement. 'You must have been a bright student, Kate. It's some switch...from art to medicine. What brought it about? Family pressure? Peer pressure? Parental expectations? You have doctors in your family?'

She sat up abruptly, causing the ice-pack to spin from his feather-light grasp and land in her lap. Snatching it up, she pressed it into her bruised flesh with fingers far less gentle than his.

'No one pressured me...I *wanted* to do medicine!' She couldn't meet Jack's eye. She was afraid that if she did, it would all tumble out...how and why Charlotte had died...how shattered her parents had been, her father in particular...how her father had vented his fury on his daughter's absent ex-lover, tearing up the note of condolence Jonathan Savage had sent from America after Charlotte's death, and throwing it away in disgust.

No...she couldn't bring herself to tell Jack all that. She was afraid tears would tumble out along with the words, and she didn't want to cry in front of Jack, didn't want to bring a sad note into their brief time together...or, worse, make him uncomfortable. Some men tended to back away from tragedy and emotion...from emotional females in particular...and she didn't want Jack backing away from *her*.

'But you still find time to do some sketching...' Jack's voice splintered her fevered thoughts.

She peeked up at him through her lashes, relief whooshing through her that he hadn't pressed her for an answer, that he'd switched from the subject of medicine. He was eyeing her sketchbook again, she noted, with a rush of heat to her cheeks.

'May I take a look?'

Alarm flared in her eyes as he reached down and picked it up.

'No!' she cried, her cheeks positively flaming now. The ice-pack, forgotten, slipped from her fingers onto the grass. 'Please, Jack—'

He laughed. It was obvious he thought she was just teasing him, or being coy. 'I won't criticise, I promise. I can't draw a straight line myself.' He flipped it open before she could stop him.

Dismay, humiliation, washed over her as a slow smile spread across his face.

'So...you did see me.' His lips stretched wider. 'From more than one angle, it seems.'

She wished she could sink through the banana lounger into oblivion. She'd more than just 'seen' him—she'd memorised every powerful sinew and tautly packed muscle of his fantastic body. She'd never been more mortified in her life!

'They're very detailed sketches.' He eyed them clinically. 'You have…an amazingly acute eye.'

'You said you wouldn't criticise,' she whispered faintly.

'I'm not criticising. I have nothing but praise.' He glanced up at her, pinning her with the glittering force of his gaze, a self-deprecating smile curving his lips. 'I'm commenting from a purely artistic point of view, you understand, not on the subject matter. You're good, Kate. Very good. You have talent.'

'You said you know nothing about art.' she reminded him, brushing off the unwanted accolade.

'I said I couldn't draw a straight line, not that I knew nothing about art.'

'Please, Jack…give it to me.' She plucked the sketchbook from his fingers and closed it firmly. 'It was just a bit of fun, and—and you were the only one on the beach…'

She flung her legs over the side of the lounger, glancing at her watch as she sat up. 'Is *that* the time? I'd better fly,' she gabbled. 'The police must have been and gone by now and my—my friend could be looking for me.' She snatched up her beach-bag and scrambled to her feet.

Jack rose too. 'I could do with another run. I'll come down to the beach with you…if that's where you're heading. You could introduce me to your friend.'

He wanted to meet Diana? Kate was shocked—disgusted—at the flash of pure jealousy that knifed through her. Diana was closer to Jack's age, and a sophisticated, high-powered woman of the world. Compared with a lowly medical student, not yet twenty…

'I—I think I'll head back to the house,' she gulped out. 'Di will probably still be there, cleaning up the mess.' If there was a police car parked outside the house she could always turn back…and hopefully meet up with Jack again down on the beach. *Alone*…just the two of them. 'Jack…thank you.' She turned to face him. 'I…my eye's feeling a lot better. Is it still swollen?'

She raised her face for his scrutiny. And felt a tingling weakness in her legs as his gaze scorched over her flushed skin.

'Not as much,' Jack assured her. His voice, warm and velvet-soft, brushed over her like a physical caress. 'But I think you should get a story ready, if you don't want your friend knowing that a strange man walloped you in the face while you were caught in a dangerous rip.'

She gave an embarrassed laugh. 'At least—thanks to you turning up, Jack—I won't have to tell her I went swimming on my own.' She could hardly hide the fact that she'd been for a swim—one glance at her damp, tangled curls would give her away. 'I know it's not quite the truth, but…' She reached out involuntarily to touch his arm. 'Thank you, Jack, for—' she caught her breath at the feel of the smooth, hard flesh under her fingers '—for saving my life.'

She felt her gaze swallowed by a blue more brilliant than the sea. 'The pleasure was all mine.' He took her uptilted chin in his hand, bent his head and kissed her. Full on the lips.

'It's not every day a fellow has the chance to pluck a golden mermaid from the sea,' he drawled as he drew back.

She couldn't move or speak for a second. She could feel her face burning, her heart thudding, her lips tingling from the brief, unexpected touch of his lips. Warm, firm, yet deliciously sensual lips, the kind of lips you wanted to go on kissing you for ever.

She saw something in his face, a fleeting glint in his eye, a deepening of the sharp blue, as if he'd surprised himself by kissing her. *Or by feeling the same spark of awareness that she'd felt?*

'I thought your eyes were grey,' he murmured with a slow smile, his voice breaking the spell. 'But they're green…as green as the sea on a wintry day.'

Was *that* what had surprised him? The colour of her eyes? She felt a ripple of disappointment. Maybe he'd felt nothing at all.

'And as beautiful,' he added softly, his fingers caressing the soft skin of her throat, his hypnotic eyes still holding hers.

Kate stared back at him, her lips trembling, parting under his gaze. She felt light-headed, breathless, as if she were floating. She couldn't drag her eyes from his. Didn't want to.

Caught up in the enchantment of the moment, dazed by a dreamy sense of unreality, she blurted something utterly unexpected, utterly unplanned. And utterly outrageous.

'You realise, don't you, Jack, that when you save someone's life…you're bound to them for ever?'

She caught her breath as the impetuous words left her lips, wishing she could snatch them back. Bound *for ever*? What in the world was she saying, thinking of? If there were any words more likely to drive a man away…!

She gave a startled jerk as Jack reached out to slide a hand round her neck under her curls, gently urging her face closer to his, his fingers warm and tinglingly intimate on her skin.

'Then maybe we ought to seal those bonds between us...with a *proper* kiss,' he suggested in a strangely husky voice.

'Jack, I didn't—'

His lips stopped her. Those warm, sumptuous lips that she'd tasted a moment ago and longed to taste again. Lips that she couldn't resist, didn't want to resist, that caused her own to melt under their gentle, seeking pressure, all thought scattering to the four winds.

Still kissing her, he slid an arm round her waist, pulling her against his muscled warmth, his powerful thighs brushing her bare legs.

Instead of feeling trapped, or in any way alarmed, she clutched at his arms and pressed even closer, elated and intoxicated by the increasing hunger of his kiss and the erratic beat of his heart against hers.

He drew back just far enough to murmur against her lips, 'You're not one of those irresistible sirens of the sea, I trust, who lure men to their destruction on the rocks?'

She gave a gurgle of husky laughter. 'Oh, Jack, I'd never do anything to hurt *you*...ever. You saved my life!' Gulping in a much needed breath, she whispered, 'Maybe we were *fated* to meet.'

'Maybe we were.' His fingers threaded through her mass of golden curls, his eyes a dark glitter above hers. 'You're already threatening to turn my life upside-down...do you realise that?'

She *was*? Kate let out a dreamy sigh as his mouth

captured hers again, preventing her from telling him that he was doing the same to her. As if he didn't know it already!

Her mind spun as his tongue slid between her teeth and began an erotic dance with hers, his lips sucking, tasting, sending a delicious fire through her veins. So this was what a *proper* kiss was…this was how it felt. Nothing like the arrogant, insensitive assaults or the clumsy, eager smooches that she'd known before…none of which had affected her in the slightest, except to fill her with a mild distaste. This was so different…the way it made her feel…wanting more…far more.

Her breath quickened as she felt his hand brush over the swell of her breast, her body arching involuntarily, her senses reeling at the intimate touch, at the exquisite sensations flaming through her. She didn't think of protesting, or drawing back. She was paralysed, lost to all reality, conscious only of the heady exhilaration of being in his arms, and the blinding realisation that he wanted her as much as she wanted him.

As a shiver of pure excitement quivered through her, Jack wrenched his mouth from hers, almost brutally pushing her back, away from him. 'My God, what am I doing? What am I letting *you* do to me?'

The magic spell shattered. Only the hands still holding her arms prevented Kate's legs from sagging beneath her. Blood rushed to her face, tears of hurt and shame springing to her eyes. He didn't want her after all. She was too fast, too easy. He was disgusted at himself for succumbing to…*her feminine wiles*. But not as disgusted as she felt at that moment—with herself.

What was she doing, letting a virtual stranger kiss her like that, *touch* her like that? As for telling him they were bound together for ever, just because he'd saved her life... She'd only just met him, for pity's sake! She didn't even know his full name.

'I'm sorry,' she croaked, blinking furiously. 'You— you must think—' She gave a choked sob and tried to tear herself free, clawing at his gripping hands with wild fingers. But his strong hands simply tightened round her arms, dragging her back to face him.

'You've nothing to be sorry for, Kate.' His voice was a throaty growl. 'Just be grateful I didn't take advantage of you. Heaven knows, I was tempted.'

He was? She swallowed, her bewildered gaze fluttering to his. Was he saying it was *because* he liked her so much—because he *respected* her—that he'd pushed her away? Were there still men like that around?

'Will—will I see you tomorrow?' she faltered, hiding the burning hope that she was sure must be there for him—for anyone—to see.

But what if Diana wanted to go home first thing in the morning—or even tonight—now that her beach-house had been burgled? Or what if she wanted to visit a *different* beach tomorrow—a safer beach for swimming? Or what if she didn't *want* her young friend meeting up with Jack again—a stranger she'd met on the beach? What if she wanted to keep Kate to herself?

As she waited for Jack's answer, Kate felt a sick ache in her chest at the thought of never seeing him again, never having the chance to know and experience more of him, never again feeling his gentle, heart-stopping touch, those powerful arms around her, those warmly sensual lips on hers.

Worse...what if she and Diana *did* meet him on the beach tomorrow, and he had eyes only for Diana?

She gave herself an impatient shake. If he was that fickle—if he could transfer his affections so easily—Diana was welcome to him! But in her heart she didn't believe he would be…not her Jack. Not the man who'd risked his life to save hers, and who'd taken such good care of her since…who'd even told her she was threatening to turn his life upside-down.

Not the man who'd had the chance to take advantage of her, who'd been tempted to, but hadn't.

'There's a woman crossing the sandhills,' Jack said suddenly, diverted for a second. He was looking beyond her through the trees. 'Is that your friend?'

Kate turned her head, following his glance. Her heart gave a flutter as she recognised the tall, slender woman striding across the grassy sand dunes…heading *back* from the beach, not towards it. It was more a flutter of guilt than dismay. Guilt that she hadn't been down on the beach when Diana had come looking for her. Guilt that she'd been enjoying herself with Jack while Diana had been dealing with the police and the aftermath of the robbery.

Guilt that she could actually have been *jealous* of Diana, even for a second! She *liked* Diana. Very much. In many ways, she liked her better than she'd liked her own sister. Besides, jealousy was such a futile, destructive emotion.

She leapt away from Jack with a gasped, 'Goodbye, Jack!' and broke into a run, leaving him standing. 'Di!' she called out, waving a hand as she emerged from the trees. 'Here I am!'

'Where have you *been*?' Diana shouted back, adding as they came closer, 'I thought you'd been kidnapped!'

Kate reddened. She had…in a way. 'Sorry, Di.' Her

teeth tugged at her lip as she came to a halt, facing the older woman. 'I...er...met someone down on the beach.' She raked her fingers through her hair, deliberately dragging her tangled curls over one eye. Her *black* eye. The longer she could hide it from Diana the better. She hadn't thought of a convincing story yet.

'And there I was, thinking you must have gone for a long walk...*on your own.*' Diana's dark eyes twinkled. 'Male or female?' she asked.

'Male.' Kate flushed. 'A real gentleman,' she said righteously. *An incredible hunk with the strength of a tank, the sexiest lips in the world, and the gentlest touch she'd ever known.*

A man she would trust with her life.

She *had* trusted him with her life.

'He wouldn't happen to be sun-tanned, dark-haired and built like an Olympic athlete, by any chance?' Diana was looking past her now, her eyes blatantly admiring.

Kate's head spun round, her cheeks blazing hot. Jack was heading their way, on his way to the beach.

'Er...yes, that's Jack.' She would have to explain a few things, quick smart. 'I...we went swimming,' she babbled, 'and he accidentally bumped me on the cheek and gave me a black eye and he—he insisted on putting an ice-pack on it, back at his...his... *Have the police been yet?*'

Diana gave an amused grin and dragged her gaze back to Kate. 'Been and gone. They say there were other reported burglaries around here a few weeks ago and it was most likely done then. The thieves have probably disposed of all the stuff by now,' she said glumly. 'At least it's all insured. Or most of it.' Her smile turned rueful. 'I'm sorry about Charlotte's briefcase, Kate. But she wasn't really keen for anyone to have it anyway.'

'No,' said Kate, sighing as she pictured the contents scattered in bushland somewhere, or abandoned in a rubbish dump or a deserted creek.

She wondered again what dark secrets her sister could have been guarding so carefully. Private, embarrassingly intimate letters? Highly personal or explicit photographs? Personal mementoes of some kind? They might have shed some more light on her sister's state of mind leading up to her death, but at the same time they could have reopened painful wounds that were only just beginning to heal. Yes, maybe it was for the best.

'Are you going to introduce me to your new friend, Kate?' Diana asked, her gaze skimming past her again. Kate saw the woman's dark eyes narrow in a frown, then widen in what looked like disbelief.

'No...it can't be,' Diana grated. 'I don't believe it.'

'Don't believe...what?' Kate glanced round.

Jack was almost upon them now. Did Diana actually know him? Her heart squeezed at the thought. Not an old lover, she begged. She wanted to think of Jack as her very own—at least while they were here at Shelly Beach—even though she knew it was crazy to imagine that she was the first woman he'd looked at in the special way he'd looked at her, the first woman he'd kissed as if it had meant something to him. He might even have used those very same words before that he'd murmured to her... *'You're already threatening to turn my life upside-down...'*

She sighed. Of course he must have had lovers. He was years older than she was, and with his looks he must have been fighting women off for years. Or *not* fighting...

Diana's gaze flickered back to hers. There was a worried frown creasing her brow. 'You don't know who he is? He didn't tell you?'

'No.' Kate's voice wobbled. Unease was curling through her, though she wasn't sure why. 'Just that his name's Jack.' Was he someone famous? Had he been kidding about being a neurosurgeon? Was he actually a famous rock star or a well-known sports star? Or a notorious playboy, known for prowling around secluded beaches?

Was that why Diana was looking worried? Because she knew he was a known womaniser, with a reputation for seducing gullible young girls?

But Jack *hadn't* seduced her. He'd been a perfect gentleman!

Well, almost.

Her fingers fluttered to her throat. Who *was* he?

As she plucked her bewildered gaze away from Diana's concerned face, Jack greeted them.

'Hi. You must be Diana.' His lips stretched in a breathtakingly attractive smile that threatened to melt Kate's bones. She hoped it wasn't affecting Diana the same way. 'I hope you weren't worried about your young friend here?'

Young friend? Kate felt a spurt of indignation. She almost snapped, I'm not a schoolkid! but something in Jack's expression stopped her. A look of growing puzzlement. A dawning frown to match Diana's.

'I've met you somewhere...haven't I?'

'That's right...Diana Morton,' the older woman said curtly. No sign of weakening knees there, Kate noted with growing unease. 'We met at a restaurant in Sydney a couple of years ago…when you were dining there with a friend of mine.'

Kate felt a steadying hand on her shoulder.

'Charlotte Warren-Smith,' Diana said evenly. 'Kate's sister.'

Kate's head snapped back. Jack had been dining with *Charlotte*? He'd known her *sister*? Her face broke out in a prickly sweat. *Don't panic!* It couldn't be *him*. Charlotte knew lots of doctors…surgeons. She could have dined with any of them.

Jack's blue eyes pierced hers. The smile had gone. She saw shocked disbelief in his eyes. 'You're Charlotte's *sister*? You can't be!' His frown deepened. 'There's no likeness whatsoever…and your name's Kate. Charlotte's sister was called…she mentioned her a few times…' He cast around for a fleeting second. 'Cathy.' As he said it, he seemed to realise the connection. Catherine… Cathy… Kate.

'Is it true?' His eyes burned into Kate's as if he still didn't believe it. Or didn't *want* to believe it. 'Charlotte's sister was still at school…she would be years younger than…how old *are* you—?' he rapped at Kate, his eyes raking over the slender, womanly curves that even the loose shirt couldn't hide.

'She's nineteen,' Diana cut in, 'and Kate *was* still at school when you knew Charlotte. Charlotte always called her sister Cathy…she was the only one who did. To everyone else she was Kate…or Catherine.'

Kate felt her stomach clenching. Why did Jack look so appalled? So shocked? A terrible suspicion was stirring, but it was a possibility she couldn't face, couldn't put into words, even in her own mind. Besides, everything screamed out that it wasn't possible.

But she had to know.

'Who are you?' Her voice was a husky croak. Without consciously realising what she was doing, she crossed her fingers.

'He's Jonathan Savage.' Again it was Diana who answered, her voice sharp, accusing, yet at the same time edged with pity. For *her*...poor, deluded, bedazzled Kate.

As the older woman voiced her worst fears, Kate went rigid with shock.

Jonathan Savage.

She felt sick. Her head whirled. She wondered how she was managing to remain standing. This was a nightmare! A cruel, living nightmare.

How could her wonderful, protective, gentle Jack be the cold-hearted, despised Jonathan Savage, the callous lover who'd broken her sister's heart and crushed her will to live? She didn't believe it. *Couldn't* believe it.

'You're wrong,' she choked out, though she was despairingly aware that Jack wasn't denying it. She swung round to face Diana. 'Jack's a *neuro*surgeon,' she cried. 'Jonathan Savage planned to be a *heart* surgeon. And he was called *Johnnie*, not Jack!'

When Diana had no answer, Kate forced herself to look up into Jack's face, still avoiding his eye, focusing all her attention on his lips, which were parting under her gaze, ready to impart the truth that would either plunge her into blackest despair or send her soaring in relief.

'Diana's right, Kate.' He spoke in a toneless, desolately cold voice that disintegrated her last dying hope.

'I *am* Jonathan Savage.' His mouth twisted. 'Charlotte was the only one who ever called me Johnnie...even though she knew I didn't care for it. To everyone else I've always been Jack...or Jonathan.'

Kate stared back at him numbly. Yes...that sounded like Charlotte. Always wanting to be different, never following the herd, forever wanting to make an impression, to be controversial, to tease.

Inside she felt as if she were dying. The wonderful Jack she'd so briefly, earth-shatteringly come to know had been a cruel illusion. He was Jonathan Savage...the man she hated most in the whole world. She steeled herself to meet the narrowed blue eyes above her. They were no longer Jack's eyes...warm, tender, smiling. They were a stranger's eyes, flat, dark, hooded, showing no emotion at all.

His voice, as cold as his eyes, washed over her, turning her veins to ice. 'I originally did plan to do heart surgery, but I switched to neurosurgery when I landed in the States.' His strong jaw jutted a trifle. 'I decided I'd be better off in neurosurgery when I came back to Australia...as I planned to do. As I still plan to do...eventually.'

Eventually, Kate noted dully. Not *soon*. No, he wouldn't want to come back soon. Not now. Not now that he knew who she was.

'Yes, I'll just *bet* you'll feel more comfortable in neurosurgery,' she breathed, balling her hands into tightly clenched fists. 'As a *heart* surgeon you might have had to come up against my father. You might even have had to work alongside him. You wouldn't have wanted to risk that. You must know how much he despises you. How much we all despise you!'

Jack's brow darkened. In a deadly quiet voice he drawled, 'Is that so?'

'Oh, don't pretend you don't know!' His coldness, his indifference incensed her. If he were showing some shame…some anguish…even an iota of feeling…it might have softened her, just a little. But he was showing none! 'You broke my sister's heart! You drove her to— to—' Her voice cracked. She wanted to pierce that cold unfeeling shell. 'You *killed* her!'

'What the hell are you talking about?' An angry red flame lit Jack's eyes. 'Your sister committed suicide. I was sorry to hear it. Shocked to hear it. But don't lay the blame at my door. I wasn't even there!'

Kate took a deep quivering breath. 'It's *because* you walked out on her that she—she took that overdose!' Her fingernails dug into her curled palms, piercing the skin, but the pain was nothing to what she felt inside. 'She loved you and couldn't bear to go on living without you!'

'That's drivel!'

Stung, as much by his denial as his lack of feeling, Kate wrenched out. 'She *told* my father how shattered she was when you walked out on her. She left a *note* before she died…and she was thinking of *you*. *"I can't live with the pain, Johnnie,"* she wrote. *Johnnie*,' she repeated meaningfully.

She clamped her mouth shut before she could add the rest. He didn't deserve to hear it. *'Forgive me'*, Charlotte had added, her overwhelming love for the man who'd left her transcending her heartache and misery. Jonathan Savage didn't deserve to know that Charlotte had been considering *his* feelings in her final moments. *He* was the one who should have been begging *her* forgiveness!

She saw Jack's eyes flare, then darken with an emotion that was impossible to read. He seemed about to say something, but drew in his lips instead, hissing in his breath, obviously thinking better of it.

Kate's eyes raked the face that only minutes ago she'd thought the most beautiful face she'd ever seen...the warmly hypnotic eyes...the sexy, enticing lips...the etched laughter lines that deepened even further when he smiled. Now she saw only coldness...withdrawal...a granite hardness. Even a vague look of...what was it? Mistrust? Derision?

A cold shiver brought goosebumps to her skin. There was going to be no softening from Jack...no apologies...no admissions. He'd closed his mind to the consequences of his heartlessness, denied all responsibility.

The Jack she'd briefly known—or thought she'd known—didn't exist.

Jack stepped back, spreading his hands. 'Well...I can see Shelly Beach isn't going to be big enough for the three of us. Goodbye, Kate.' His eyes were flat, unreadable as they briefly brushed hers. 'Diana.'

He swung on his heel and strode back the way he'd come. To pack his bags, presumably. Kate, watching him go, felt as if her heart had been ripped from her body and crushed under his feet. How would she ever be able to trust another man again? Or trust her *feelings* again?

'Good riddance,' Diana muttered. 'You're well rid of him, Kate. Arrogant, unfeeling bastard.'

Kate nodded. Arrogant...unfeeling...yes, that described Jonathan Savage. Well, he had the right attributes to become a successful, high-powered specialist surgeon, she thought with a bitter smile. And she should know. She'd seen the same attributes in her own father.

But at least her father had shown some feeling when his beloved Charlotte had died.

Jonathan Savage had shown no feeling at all.

Kate tore her eyes from his receding frame, trying to blot from her mind the powerful shoulders, the bronzed, gleaming muscles, the dark hair lifting as he moved.

She was *glad* he was leaving Shelly Beach...*glad* he was going back to America. If he decided to stay overseas for good she would be even happier. She never wanted to see him again. Ever.

She hated him.

She would always hate him.

CHAPTER FOUR

How could *he* be here? At *her* hospital?

Her eyes raked over the man facing her, her mind reeling.

Jonathan Savage!

A highly civilised, ultra-suave, smoothly self-assured Jonathan Savage, with success stamped all over his impressive, expensively clad frame.

Yet the Jack she'd briefly known was still there too, she realised shakily. The same incredibly blue eyes...the same massive shoulders...the same firm, sensual mouth. Her lips parted involuntarily.

Then tightened as she jerked back to earth, realising as she fought for her normal coolness that he'd recognised her too. She could see it in the flare of his eyes, in the narrowing that swiftly followed, in the taut lines of his face, in his slight withdrawal.

'Kate.' It was still the same deep, soft voice. But there was no joy in it, no warmth. His dismay, as he recovered from his own initial shock, was evident. 'What are *you* doing here at St Mark's?'

'I *work* here,' she said, striving to keep her voice steady, which was pretty difficult when her teeth, for some reason, were chattering like castanets. With reaction. Shock. She'd often wondered how she would react if she ever came face to face with him again. But she'd never expected to feel this shaken, this fragile, her whole body jangling with tension.

'I'm a second-year resident.' A fully fledged doctor, her eyes told him. A long way from the gullible, impressionable nineteen-year-old medical student you knew five years ago. 'I'm doing a stint in Emergency.' She flicked her gaze away from his, as if looking around for another likely car space, though it was actually to avoid having to look directly at him.

'Well...so it's *Dr* Warren-Smith now. Congratulations.' There was a cynical dryness in his tone, as if he hadn't expected anything less. 'But why are you working here at St Mark's?' A puzzled frown quirked his brow. 'I thought you would have been at Eastern General with your father...training under him.'

She nearly laughed aloud, but caught it back in time. 'Heart surgery didn't appeal,' she said shortly. She lifted her chin. Her father might still have hopes that she'd change her mind and specialise, but the hopes were dying fast—especially now that she was getting married.

She gulped, her gaze fluttering back to his. Would he be surprised if he knew? Would he *care*? Feel the faintest pang of regret? No...*hardly*. That brief spark of tenderness he'd once felt for her—that ever-so-fleeting blaze of passion—had died the moment he'd found out who she was. And vice versa... Her own passion dying just as quickly when she'd learned who *he* was.

She considered waving her left hand under his nose, so that he would see her engagement ring and *know*. Then remembered it was at the jeweller's, being altered. It had been slightly loose and she'd been worried about losing it.

'And what about *you*, Dr Savage?' she asked, rallying—though her voice was still lamentably husky—far huskier than normal. 'Are you a fully-fledged neurosurgeon now? You—you're not working here at St Mark's...are you?' she faltered, and surreptitiously crossed her fingers. With a bit of luck he was only paying a visit. Maybe a friend of his was a patient here.

But he couldn't be a private visitor. He wouldn't have access to the doctors' car park. She swallowed. Hard.

'Yes, to both questions.' His eyes, when she flicked another veiled glance up at him, were as hooded as her own. 'I've been appointed assistant neurosurgeon to Magnus Barratt. He's Australia's top brain surgeon, as I'm sure you know. I've an office and consulting rooms here at St Mark's.'

She felt dizzy. How could they both work at the same hospital? How could she bear it? How could *he*, knowing how much she despised him...knowing that she blamed him for her sister's death? Was he hoping that after all this time she might have forgiven him? Or even *forgotten* his callous treatment of her sister and its tragic consequences?

Or didn't he care, one way or the other? No...Jonathan Savage wouldn't care about the feelings of anyone—even those of his patients, she wouldn't be surprised—let alone care about a lowly hospital resident...one he could easily avoid in a hospital the size of St Mark's. Unless she had to do a stint *under* him, as part of her training.

She shuddered, imagining how he'd be likely to treat her if she did. The same way some of the more arrogant specialists took pleasure in doing. Deliberately questioning everything she did...deliberately challenging her...trying to find fault...simply because she was a Warren-Smith. And a female. Jonathan Savage would have even more reason than most to victimise her, if he still held a grudge against her for accusing him of causing her sister's death.

'By the way, I don't call myself Jonathan Savage any more.' His drawling voice cut through her fretful thoughts. 'I've been Jack Savage for some time now. Dr Jack Savage.'

She blinked, surprised that an ambitious, high-powered neurosurgeon would prefer to call himself Jack rather than the more lofty, formal Jonathan.

Her eyes narrowed. Unless it was to escape the stigma of the name *Jonathan Savage*. He must know that her father and some of his closest colleagues—Sydney's medical élite—had pointed the finger of blame at *him* for the shock suicide of Chester Warren-Smith's brilliant elder daughter. Her father had made *sure* they knew!

Why, Kate wondered with a frown, would Jack Savage want to come back to practise here in Sydney, when he must know there could still be whispers and conjecture surrounding him? To show people he didn't care? To prove that he could reach the top, regardless of innuendo and rumours?

Or simply because Sydney was his home town, and he was determined to defy anyone who wanted to keep him away?

She remembered the time and gasped, 'I have to be on duty at three! C-can we settle this later? I have to find a carspace and dash!'

Jack looked pointedly at his watch. 'There was little chance of you making it on time, Doctor, even before you careered into me.'

She flushed. He made it sound as if she made a habit of being late. Of being irresponsible.

'Or is it simply that, being a Warren-Smith, you feel you're above the rules?' he added silkily.

Her eyes snapped to his. Before she could stop herself she was lashing back at him. 'You have the hide to criticise my family after what *you* did to us? After what you did to my sister?'

He didn't even flinch. A cold veil descended over the vivid blue eyes. 'I had hoped,' he said levelly, 'that after all this time you would have ceased that tiresome refrain. I don't accept any blame for your sister's death, and never did. Charlotte was her own woman. She made her own decisions, for her own reasons, and acted accordingly. I don't believe she would have allowed me or any other man to influence her life…let alone to that extent.'

He paused, before adding in the same toneless voice. 'And I very much doubt that she deliberately took her own life…that she meant to go…that far.'

Kate's mouth gaped. But she had no chance to set him straight, no chance to lash back at him for his heartless, blinkered misreading of the situation. He was already reminding her, 'But you have to dash off.' He lifted a mocking eyebrow. 'Just wait till I move my car, will you, before you go racing off to new parking spot? We don't want another collision.'

As she stood seething he stepped away. She caught the sardonic smile on his lips as he rapped over his shoulder, 'No need to exchange details now, Dr Warren-Smith. I'll know where to find you.'

That sounded ominous, she thought, stomping back to her own car. He obviously wasn't going to forget that *she'd* caused the damage to his car. Thank heaven she was insured!

Before climbing into her car she shot back, 'I'm

known as Dr *Smith* here at St Mark's.' She lifted her chin a notch. 'Warren-Smith is too much of a mouthful.' As well as being a name that haunted her wherever she went...a highly recognisable name that tended to alienate some people and make others jealous, or kowtow to her, or expect too much of her. 'Luckily, I'm the only Dr Smith here.'

She could hardly wait until the day she changed her name to Kate Armstrong.

A tremor ran through her as she remembered Brendan. She hadn't even thought of him, she realised contritely, since Jack Savage's shock appearance.

She cast one last final glance back before twitching herself down in the driver's seat. Her throwaway statement about her name appeared to have surprised him. He'd paused for a second, his eyes boring across the distance between them. It was only when their eyes clashed that he swung round and disappeared into his dented BMW. With a low roar the car lunged forward.

Of course... Her mouth curled. He'd be anxious to get his car safely out of her way!

For the rest of the afternoon, until well into the evening, she expected Jack Savage to come bearing down on her, demanding details of her insurance company and her address, and whatever else was required to set into motion the repair of his car. She jumped every time a tall figure appeared. But it was never him. He must have gone home, she decided finally.

Contrarily, she found herself *wanting* him to appear. Not that she wanted to spend any more time with him...heavens no! She simply wanted to set him straight on a few things. He was burying his head in the sand where Charlotte's death was concerned and she wasn't going to let him get away with it! He had to face up to what he'd done to her sister. She wanted him to *feel* something—guilt, remorse, pity, anything—and to accept at least some responsibility. She would never be able to *begin* to forgive him until he did. If she ever could.

She sighed, wishing she were on day shift, so that she could spend her evenings—or at least the occasional evening—with Brendan. She was hardly seeing him at all at the moment. By the time she finished work, around midnight, he was already in bed at his family home, sound asleep. He needed his sleep, he'd often told her, so that he could function properly during the day. His work was very important to him.

She'd never actually missed Brendan before, that she could remember, but she was missing him badly now, she realised. She hadn't even spoken to him on the phone today. There hadn't been a chance. He normally rang her in his lunch break, but today she'd gone out to lunch with Melanie, and from there to Madame Yvette's.

She sighed. Didn't he realise how much she needed him? Couldn't he *sense* her need?

She had to smile at that…at the thought that Brendan might actually sense her psychic vibes. He was a sensible, rational, down-to-earth guy. Not the sort to indulge in extra-sensory perception!

A white-coated figure brushed past the bed-trolley where she was examining a patient. Her head snapped round, her whole body tingling with tension. But it wasn't Jack Savage. Her breath whooshed out, her brow furrowing in exasperation. Of course it wouldn't be him. None of the patients in here tonight had any need for a neurosurgeon. And he would hardly accost her about a car park bingle while she was with a patient.

She realised her hands were shaking. What was *wrong* with her? She'd never felt so screamingly on edge in her life!

Around eight o'clock she took time off to grab a bite to eat in the hospital canteen, holding her breath as she walked in. But he wasn't there either. The few resident doctors who were there, though, were talking about him. Or the *female* residents were.

'He's gorgeous,' raved Georgia, from Paediatrics, pulling back a chair for her as she joined them. 'And he's single, can you believe that?'

'When he looks at you with those eyes,' Ella sighed dreamily, 'you just want to die. Or do anything he asks.'

'Have you seen our new neurosurgeon yet, Kate?' Georgia winked at her. 'His name's Jack Savage—and oh, boy, I'll bet he's a real savage in bed.' She rolled her eyes. 'He's built like a—like a—'

'Like a Greek god?' Kate said helpfully. 'He wasn't so god-like when I crashed into his car in the car park this afternoon.'

'Oh, Kate you didn't? How did *that* happen?'

'I backed into him. My fault.' Kate shrugged. 'I was running late and wasn't looking.'

'You mean he bawled you out…a beautiful dreamboat like Dr Savage?' Georgia's eyes widened.

Kate grimaced. 'I made quite a dent in his car.'

'You're saying a wealthy bigshot like Dr Jack Savage is going to make you pay up?' put in one of the male residents with a sympathetic grin.

'We didn't have time to settle the details.' Kate gave another shrug as she picked up her fork and bent over her plate. 'I suppose he'll come chasing after me to-morrow, demanding his pound of flesh.'

She'd meant to dismiss Jack Savage with a nonchalant throwaway line, but the word 'flesh' raised a startling image of bronzed naked skin, which in turn brought a prickly flush to her cheeks. To cover up, she pulled a face and muttered, 'He doesn't seem the type who'd let a girl off.' She preferred to paint him as the ogre he was rather than the benevolent heart-throb they seemed to think him.

'So you're not impressed.' Georgia eyed her thoughtfully. 'Even though you're blushing.'

'I'm not!' Kate denied, flushing more than ever. 'It was—it was embarrassing, that's all.'

'Of course Kate's not blushing,' Ella defended her. 'She's engaged to be married. She'll be walking down the aisle in a couple of weeks!'

'No woman, single or attached, could be immune to this man,' Georgia intoned. 'Look, as nice as your Brendan is, Kate—and he'll make a perfect husband, I'm sure, who'll never put a foot wrong—he doesn't hold a candle to Jack Savage in the looks and build department. Or the charisma department either. Sorry, but it's true.'

'Georgia!' Ella rebuked. 'It's what's underneath that matters, not the dressing on the outside. Don't listen to her, Kate. Brendan is a nice-looking guy. He's nice all the way through.'

'Maybe Dr Savage is nice all the way through too,' Georgia suggested. 'I'd love to find out.' She licked her lips.

Kate was tempted to set her straight as to what Dr Savage was like underneath his heart-stopping exterior, but she bit back the bitter words in time. Unlike her father, she'd never mentioned Jonathan Savage's name in connection with her sister's death. She'd never even talked about the tragedy, and her friends had respected her silence on the subject. She was glad now that she hadn't. If she had to work in the same hospital as Dr Savage, it was far better that nobody knew what lay behind the antagonism between them. If anyone sensed it in the days to come, they could always put it down to their car park altercation.

She remained on edge for the rest of the evening, even when she left the hospital shortly after midnight to head for the car park before driving home to the flat she shared with Melanie. She saw no sign of Jack Savage on her way out.

She breathed a sigh of relief...even though she knew that tomorrow, if he didn't seek her out first, or call her on the phone, she would have to seek *him* out.

'Kate, what are you doing here?' Georgia waved a hand as Kate walked into the hospital canteen around midday the next day. 'Are you back on day shift?'

'Not till next week,' Kate said with a smile. 'No, I had some work to catch up on.' She glanced round to see if Jack Savage was there. He wasn't. No...he'd have his meals taken to him in his suite, no doubt. Or he'd swan off to a club or restaurant with one of his specialist cronies.

He hadn't rung her or left a message demanding to see her, which puzzled her a little. Surely he'd want to settle things and get his car fixed as quickly as possible. She chewed on her lip. There was something *she* wanted to settle with him too, something far more important. At the thought of it her heartbeat quickened and she had to take some quick gulps of air.

After lunch, unable to stand the suspense and the waiting around, she went looking for him. Or at least she made some discreet enquiries about his whereabouts, pretending she had a message for him.

She found out he was operating. He'd started early that morning and would be in the OR until late afternoon. She grimaced, mentally conceding that she probably owed him an apology. But it was nowhere near the apology he owed her, she thought, rallying. She stood sighing a moment. *Now* what was she going to do? By the time he finished operating she would be back on duty.

Taking a deep breath, she pulled out her notepad and scribbled a note asking to see him privately at a time suitable to him. She signed it *'Dr Kate Smith'*. After placing it in his pigeon-hole, she headed for the library to do some reading until she went on duty at three.

During the afternoon, and even longer evening, she half expected him to turn up in the ER and pluck her aside in full view of the other staff, which wouldn't have suited her at all. It would be impossible to broach the subject uppermost in her mind unless she saw him in private. She wasn't sure if she was relieved or disappointed when he didn't appear.

It was nearly one o'clock before she came off duty. That wasn't unusual…she seldom finished on the dot of midnight. Before leaving the hospital she checked her internal mail. Among the memos and brochures was a note from Jack Savage. *'My office. Midnight.'*

Her heart fluttered. He was still here? He wanted to see her *now*? No, not now, she realised with a groan.

Nearly an hour ago. If she'd found his note earlier she might have been able to get to his office on time. She could have told the other doctors on duty that Dr Savage the neurosurgeon wanted to see her. Had he waited? Or given up in exasperation?

She removed her white coat, grabbed her handbag, and headed for his office. The door was closed. And locked too, she'd be prepared to bet. He hadn't bothered to wait. And she couldn't blame him, at this hour. Anyone would be worn out after doing delicate brain surgery all day.

She knocked, without much hope.

'Come in.'

Her heart leapt to her mouth. He was still here! She flicked her tongue over her lips, took a deep breath, and opened the door.

He was sitting, not behind his desk, but in one of the two deep leather armchairs, with a sheaf of notes in his hand. She blinked under the bright fluorescent lights. He was still working!

'I'm sorry,' she heard herself blurting out breathlessly. 'I only found your note when I came off duty. It's been a busy night and—'

'There's no need to apologise, Dr…Smith. I'm a doctor too, you know. I know what emergency departments are like.' He waved her to the armchair opposite. 'Take a seat.'

'Thank you.' She perched on the edge of the chair, hitching her skirt down as far as she could—wishing she'd worn one that covered her knees—before raising her eyes to face him.

As she felt the full force of his glittering blue eyes, far closer now than in the car park yesterday—alarmingly close, in fact—tiny shock waves jack-knifed through her.

For a timeless, breathless second she found herself staring back at him, transfixed by his sharply compelling gaze, acutely aware of every tiny fleck in the brilliant blue, each dark curling eyelash.

Moistening her lips, she blinked to break the contact and willed her voice to work normally. If the husky croak that came out was normal! 'I—I've written down the name of my insurance company for you.' She fumbled in her handbag, avoiding the penetrating gaze. 'They—they'll handle everything.' She held the scrap of paper out to him, noting in dismay that her hand was shaking. 'I've written down my home address and phone number as well.'

He made no move to take it from her. '*That's* what you wanted to see me about? Our little bingle in the car park?' He waved her hand away and sat back, a sardonic smile on his lips. 'Forget it. It's all fixed. I had it repaired this morning.'

'B-but…' She swallowed. 'Doesn't your insurance company want—?'

'I didn't do it through my insurance company. And I don't need yours to be involved either. It wasn't worth it. It was a minor dent, easily fixed.'

'You mean…you paid cash? How much was it?' she demanded, trying to hide her dismay. Even a minor dent could cost hundreds—thousands, in some cases she'd heard about—which mightn't be much to him, but *she* didn't have that kind of money at her fingertips. She was a low-paid resident on a budget. If he thought she received an allowance from her father and could afford to pay cash, he was mistaken. She'd always refused her father's help, taking on extra jobs during her student days at uni to make ends meet.

'I think that's my business, don't you?' he drawled. 'It needn't concern you.'

'But if I'm to pay you—'

'Have I *asked* you to pay?'

She blinked at him. 'But of course I must pay. It was my fault!'

His eyebrows shot up. She wasn't sure if his expression was one of surprise or mockery. 'Well, it's nice to know that you're eager to part with your undoubted largesse...' *Mockery*, she thought tightly. 'But I suggest you keep it for the next car you bump into. The driver next time might not be so forgiving.'

Her eyes flashed, her hands clenching again. 'I don't need your forgiveness,' she snapped. 'If anyone needs forgiveness, it's you!' She sucked in her breath. She hadn't meant to say that, it had slipped out. But she didn't retract it. She shifted on the edge of her chair, the real reason she'd come to see him trembling on her lips.

'Do you have something else to say, Dr Smith?' he asked, lifting a languid eyebrow. 'You might as well spit it all out.' He glanced at his watch. 'But don't take too long...I do want to get home some time.'

'Yes, I do have something to say!' She gulped in another breath. 'I...you're deluding yourself about Charlotte's death,' she said in a rush. 'It wasn't accidental. It wasn't even a cry for help. She *meant* to end her life!'

He pursed his lips. 'If you say so. I beg to differ, that's all.'

'*Why?*' she breathed raggedly. 'What makes you think...?' She gave an impatient twitch of her shoulder.

'Because it makes you feel better about what happened? It takes away some of your guilt? Is that it?'

'Not at all.' The cold, impassive mask was back. 'I don't believe it because I knew Charlotte.' He paused, then said evenly, 'She was a tough, hard-boiled, ruthlessly driven woman with the mind of a steel trap...not the fragile, emotional *victim* you seem to think she was. Least of all a victim of love!'

Kate stared at him, clenching her hands...even though something quivered deep inside her. She'd always believed Charlotte to be like that too. A relentlessly ambitious, intensely focused woman, determined to reach the top, no matter what she had to do to get there. But obviously she hadn't been!

'You're forgetting her note,' she ground out. 'She couldn't bear the *pain* any more, she said. And she was saying it to you...*Johnnie*, remember? Because you'd left her and she couldn't bear it. She—she even added the words *"Forgive me"*, because she didn't want you to blame yourself for—for what she was about to do. She cared that much about you!'

She saw a silvery flicker in the blue. The first faint glimmer of emotion? It was gone before she could be sure.

'Maybe she just wanted me to know that she...felt something.' His shoulders lifted and fell. His eyes were hooded again, as unreadable as ever. If there'd been any softening there, it would have been for *her*, the grieving sister, Kate suspected, not for Charlotte. 'Or maybe it was a last-ditch plea for sympathy.' His own tone was anything but sympathetic. It held a cold intensity that made her wonder who he was trying to convince. Her? Or *himself*?

Unfeeling monster!

'I still believe her death was accidental,' he persisted. 'A tragic mistake on her part. A drastic ploy—for attention, sympathy, whatever—that backfired.' He leaned towards her slightly, as if determined to press home his point, and make her believe it. 'Charlotte had everything to live for, everything going for her. She had a blazing ambition to get to the top of her field. And nothing was going to stop her.'

Kate's eyes wavered. Was *that* the reason he'd walked out on her sister? Because she'd put her work before him? Because she'd been too driven to consider anyone else? Had Charlotte only realised how much she'd loved him after he'd gone?

She shook her head, hardening her heart. If Jack Savage thought that was going to let him off the hook, he was wrong, quite wrong! 'Her death was no accident,' she insisted shakily, 'though I can understand why you'd want to believe it was...to ease your conscience!'

She snatched in a steadying breath. 'Charlotte meant to take her life...there's no question. She was a *doctor*...she knew how many pills to take. She swallowed a whole bottle full!'

'Then I'm sorry,' Jack said in a marginally softer tone, but there was no apology in his eyes. They were as remote, as cool as ever.

She sighed and stood up. The gentle, protective, teasing-eyed Jack—the Jack who'd once fooled her into believing he was everything a girl could want in a man—had gone, completely gone.

'And *I'm* sorry I've kept you up so late. Goodnight, Dr Savage.' Her eyes were as cool as his, though underneath she wasn't so cool. Her stomach was still churning, her heartbeat too rapid, her nerves on edge. What he'd said about Charlotte had shaken her. While she still blamed him for her sister's death, maybe he hadn't been as deliberately heartless as she and her family had believed. Maybe he *hadn't* known how deeply Charlotte had felt about him.

He rose too, throwing his papers on the desk. 'Have you called for the security guard yet?' he asked as she turned towards the door.

She paused, glancing back. Since an attack on a nurse in the car park a few weeks ago, a security guard was supposed to accompany lone female staff to their cars after dark. 'No...I usually don't bother,' she said. 'Why?'

'You should.' His tone was mildly reproving. 'I'll see you out to your car myself.' He grabbed some keys from his desk.

She swallowed. She would never have equated gentlemanly chivalry with Jonathan Savage. With *Jack*, yes...

'There's no need for—'

'I'm heading there myself.'

'OK. Thanks.' She twitched a shoulder. It was no big deal. If he was already leaving, heading for the car park himself, what else could he have said?

She walked with brisk, businesslike steps as they left the hospital together...wanting to give an impression of normality to anyone watching. Two doctors coming off duty, heading for their separate cars in the car park, anxious to get home to bed.

Bed... Her cheeks burned in the velvety darkness. Why did the thought of *bed* conjure up graphic images in her mind? Not of Brendan, her fiancé—he'd be snoring his head off by now, no doubt, in the house he shared with his father—but of a bold, piercing-eyed, golden-muscled... *No!* She mustn't even think it! She couldn't believe she was having such shockingly lurid fantasies. An engaged woman, about to be married!

And about *this* man of all men.

Besides, the reality didn't match the fantasy. Not by a long way. She cast a narrowed, furtive glance up at Jack Savage through her lashes, deliberately hardening her heart. He might be heavenly to look at...he might be a real dreamboat on the surface...but she of all people knew how deceiving looks could be. And feelings.

He couldn't affect her now. Or ever again. She only had to think of her sister.

'You live close to the hospital?' He flicked a glance round—catching *her* covert glance. Her eyelashes fluttered away.

'About fifteen minutes by car.' Her normally husky voice had taken on a peculiar squeak. Why did he want to know?

'The family home, is it?' His tone was remote again, cold-edged.

'No, it isn't.' A tartness overcame the husky squeak. Did he think she was tied to her parents' apron strings? To her father's in particular? 'I share a house with a friend.'

He absorbed that for a second, before enquiring silkily, 'Male or female?'

'That's none of your business!' she bit back, and flushed. Why did she keep reacting to him, getting so hot under the collar, letting him get under her skin? She spied her car ahead. It was like a lifeline. She quickened her steps. 'Where are *you* living?' she shot back. Not that she wanted to know. It was simply to divert *his* questions.

'I've a flat at Rose Bay.' He'd lengthened his stride to keep up. 'I don't share it with anybody,' he added in the same silky drawl. 'At least...not yet.'

'Well, I'm sure it won't be long before you find someone,' she heard herself whipping back—and was horrified at her waspish tone, and the odd twinge she'd felt as she said it. She was so disgusted with herself that she lashed out at him with all the scorn she could muster. 'I'm sure you haven't lost your knack for picking up susceptible females!'

'Ah...' A mocking *ah*, that sent shivers down her spine. 'So you haven't completely forgotten how you allowed yourself to be picked up at one time by a strange man on a deserted beach...'

She faltered, her cheeks flaming. Her car, she saw with a whoosh of relief, was only a few steps away now. She fumbled for her keys, trying to blot his voice out.

'A stranger you sketched in lurid detail...a stranger you allowed to kiss you...a stranger—'

'*Stop!*' She whirled round. 'I don't ever want to be reminded of that day! I don't ever want to be reminded of what a fool I was...thinking I *knew* you, thinking I could trust you...' Her voice cracked, which made her more furious than ever. His great bulk was a looming shadow, the lamplight picking up the wicked glint in his eye, adding to her quivering tension.

'Good*night*, Dr Savage...' She yanked her car door open, and forced out, 'Thanks for seeing me to my car. Next time I'll take your advice and make sure I ask a security guard to accompany me!'

She was revving the engine even before she'd closed

the car door. Aware there were no other cars around, she didn't even bother to look behind her to ensure he was out of her way before she backed out—though she did catch sight of him a moment later as she roared off.

He was standing well away from the spot where she'd backed out—and he seemed to be shaking his head. And *grinning*.

The fire in her deflated. Her face was still burning, but it was from chagrin now. What a complete fool she'd made of herself! To lose control like that...to let her feelings get the better of her. Coolness... indifference...that was the only way to deal with Jack Savage.

She must treat him in future the same way he treated her sister's memory. With utter, absolute indifference.

CHAPTER FIVE

SHE woke early, after a restless, far too short sleep. She might have tried to drop off to sleep again, only she wanted to call Brendan, hoping to catch him at home before he left for the office.

'Kate! What are you doing ringing me at this hour?' He sounded a bit distracted, as he always did when pressed for time. He hated being late, so much so that he normally arrived far too early wherever he went. 'Is something wrong? Why aren't you still asleep?'

'Nothing's wrong. I just haven't spoken to you for a couple of days.' She heaved a sigh. 'I wondered if you'd like to meet me for lunch.'

'Oh, love, I'm sorry. I already have a lunch appointment. It's business, so I can't get out of it.'

'No, of course not.' She sighed again. 'Never mind, I'll grab some lunch at the Art Gallery. I'm planning to pop in to see the Archibald Exhibition later this morning.'

'Good idea.' Brendan wasn't interested in art, not even her own, though he made admiring noises whenever she showed him a sketch or portrait she'd laboured over at her weekly art class—though he quickly brushed over any nude sketches.

Brendan had a hobby of his own—stamp collecting—which she tolerated in the same way he tolerated her art. He was into stamps in a big way. He attended regular meetings and even went to stamp fairs and competed in exhibitions.

'Well…I'll see you Saturday,' she said. She had a rare weekend off. 'My mother wants us to start work on the seating arrangements for the wedding.' She grimaced. A great way to spend a day off, she thought.

'Er…can't you and your mother do that?' Brendan ventured. 'Or can't we just leave it to your parents?'

'You don't care where your friends and relatives sit? Or who with?'

'Well, no…not really. I trust you, darling,' he said warmly. A little *too* warmly. 'And I trust your parents.'

She had a suspicious feeling he wasn't telling her something. 'Is there something else you'd rather do on Saturday?' she asked. 'Or something you want me to do with you?' It suddenly hit her. '*I* know!' she said, a teasing smile in her voice. 'You want to have a bucks' night after all. And you want to sleep all day preparing for it!'

'No!' he denied emphatically. 'Bucks' nights are out. They're just an excuse to get sloshed.' Brendan hated getting drunk, losing control, being the butt of jokes. She'd suggested he spend a quiet evening at home instead, with his closest mates, but he'd refused that too, thinking it still might get out of hand.

'Kate… I…um…' He stopped and started again. 'Darling, would you mind terribly if I, um, went away this weekend?' He went on in a rush, 'I've been invited to a weekend stamp fair in Melbourne. They want me to be a judge.' His voice throbbed with pride. 'It's the first time I've been asked. I know I shouldn't go, so close to the wedding, but…' He paused, waiting for her to reassure him.

She didn't disappoint him. 'Of course you must go. What an honour! A *judge*. Brendan, that's wonderful.' She wondered when he'd planned to tell her. On his way to the airport? But that was unfair. He'd probably only decided last night, and had intended to call her later this morning. Brendan didn't have an irresponsible bone in his body. *She* was the irresponsible one, often forgetting to tell him where she would be at any given time, or what she'd be doing.

She flushed, remembering Jack Savage. Would it be irresponsible of her not to mention to Brendan—or to her parents, more to the point—that he was back in town, working at *her* hospital? It wouldn't mean much to Brendan, even if he'd heard her father growl the name Jonathan Savage at some time or other in connection with his older daughter's death. Brendan had never even known Charlotte.

She'd certainly never mentioned Jonathan Savage's name to Brendan…let alone that she'd met him, briefly and tumultuously, five years ago.

As for her father, let him find out through the medical grapevine that Jonathan Savage was back in town. Learning from his peers that Dr Jack Savage, as he was calling himself now, had become a respected neurosurgeon, assisting the top man in Sydney, might defuse the explosion that was likely if her father heard it from *her*, a member of his family. It was seven years since Charlotte's suicide, and, whatever Kate's own opinion of Jack Savage, Jack didn't deserve to be victimised, after all this time, for his role in her sister's death.

It surprised her a little that she'd come to this conclusion.

'I knew you wouldn't mind, Kate.' Brendan was

beaming—she could hear it in his voice. 'Maybe we could have lunch tomorrow...Friday. Oh, no I can't,' he groaned. 'I'm flying to Melbourne on the five o'clock flight, which means I'll need to leave work early. I was going to skip lunch to make up for it.' Brendan was punctilious about working his full eight-hour day. 'Unless you'd like a quick bite in the office? I could send out for something.'

'Brendan, I can't. I have my art class tomorrow,' she reminded him, aware of a flicker of relief. A rushed take-away lunch in Brendan's office was not an appealing prospect. Especially as he would probably go on working while she was with him.

'Oh, yes, I forgot.' His own relief was palpable. Now he wouldn't have to waste any time at all. 'Darling, I'm sorry. I'll make it up to you,' he promised.

'I know you will.' She knew he meant it. He was the most considerate, most well-intentioned man in the world. And the most reliable. It wasn't his fault that something always seemed to come up—work demands, art classes, family, friends, or his own stamp meetings—to spoil their plans. More often than not it was her own fault. Her hours were hellish, her workload murder.

'We'll catch up next week,' she said brightly. 'I'll be back on day shift Monday.'

'You're an angel, Kate. Let's have dinner Monday night so I can tell you all about the stamp fair. We could ask Mel to join us...she'd be interested too. Darling, let's have dinner every night next week,' he offered expansively.

'Yes, let's,' Kate said, knowing it would never happen. They were both far too busy, and with the wedding so close there was bound to be something that needed doing...though her mother was happy to do most of it, now that she was only working part-time at her medical clinic.

'If only you weren't on night shift *this* week,' Brendan lamented, though she could tell by his voice that he was becoming distracted again, anxious to leave for work. 'Never mind...in a couple of weeks you'll be mine for a whole fortnight. Better go, darling. Bye.'

'Bye, darling,' she murmured as the phone clicked in her ear. *'Mine for a whole fortnight...'* He was talking about their honeymoon in Hawaii, of course, but he could just as well have said, *Mine for the rest of our lives.*

For the first time, the word 'mine' struck her as frighteningly real. And frighteningly permanent.

In one of the great halls of Sydney's Art Gallery, Kate stood staring up at a life-size nude self-portrait of Selwyn Dodd, the renowned portrait painter...winner of the prestigious Archibald portrait prize, announced a week ago. Unlike Selwyn's more conventional portraits, this was a flamboyantly impressionistic painting, with swirls of colour and exaggerated lines and squiggles blurring the reclining figure.

It really looked nothing like the Selwyn Dodd she knew! Not that she'd ever seen Selwyn in the nude. Selwyn, though only in his thirties and in reasonable physical shape, never modelled for his students himself, always using hired models.

'The nude male form still fascinates you?'

Her head jerked round at the sound of the deep soft voice from behind, shock clogging her throat. A pair of laughing blue eyes met her startled gaze.

Jack Savage!

'What are you doing here?' Attack, she thought, is the best defence. 'I wouldn't have thought art shows were your thing.' Her heart was thrashing about in her chest like a fish out of water. *The nude male form...* So he hadn't forgotten that unfortunate semi-nude sketch of him that she'd done five years ago.

'I might not be able to draw to save myself,' he conceded, 'but I've been an avid art collector for years.'

A *collector*? She eyed him narrowly. Purely for investment purposes, she was prepared to bet, not out of any genuine love or sheer enjoyment of art. Quite a few of her father's specialist cronies were avid art collectors too, who bought and sold paintings purely for cold-nosed profit. Jack Savage—already a member of the élite boys' club, and heading for the top of his exalted field—had obviously jumped early onto the asset-building bandwagon.

'Are you only interested in the Archibald prize winner, or are you here to inspect all the entries?' she asked, a mock sweetness only barely masking her cynicism.

'I've cast an eye over them all, but this was the one I was particularly interested in.'

The winner. Naturally. 'I guess you'll be wanting to buy a Selwyn Dodd original now, after all the publicity and hype he's been getting?' Her eyes mocked him. 'His paintings are already worth a small fortune, but with this big prize under his belt, his prices will soar. Be prepared to pay through the nose.'

'I already own a couple of Selwyn Dodds,' Jack smoothly informed her. 'I bought them when Selwyn was just starting out—years ago, before anyone knew him. I'm always keen to encourage new talent.' The blue eyes glinted meaningfully, and she swallowed, remembering how he'd told her that *she* had talent five years ago.

She brushed off the memory, focusing on what else he'd just said, surprised to hear that he already owned a couple of Selwyn's paintings. He must know more about art than she'd thought, if he'd been able to see that Selwyn showed promise years ago, before he became wealthy and famous.

'Well, your paintings must be worth a fortune now,' she said with a shrug. He must be delighted. 'Are you going to sell them, or hang on to them?'

His mouth twisted a little—almost, she thought with a testy frown, as if he believed that was what *she* would want to do.

'I didn't buy them with the expectation of making money out of them,' he said evenly. 'I bought them because Selwyn's a friend of mine and I believe in encouraging my friends. His early paintings happen to mean a lot to me. I have no intention of parting with them. In fact, he painted one of them specially *for* me.'

Her eyes widened. 'You *know* Selwyn?' She wouldn't have thought Selwyn Dodd was Dr Jack Savage's type. An unconventional, free-living artist who mixed with the bohemian set. A *penniless* artist only a few years ago, when Jack had last been in Sydney.

'I went to school with him,' Jack said shortly. His eyes probed hers. 'You called him Selwyn...as if *you* know him.'

'He's my art teacher.' She didn't flinch under his searching gaze, though she was aware of a quickening in her heartbeat, a dryness in her mouth. 'He's teaching me life drawing and portrait painting, so I can paint passable portraits one day.'

Now *she* had surprised *him*—she could see it in his eyes—though *why* he should look so surprised puzzled her. She'd told him five years ago that she was a frustrated artist who liked to 'doodle' in her spare time.

'I thought you'd given up your artistic ambitions years ago...to concentrate on medicine,' he said, drawing her to one side to let other people admire the winning portrait.

She eyed him speculatively through her lashes, her skin prickling at the way he'd remembered so much from five years ago. Or was it prickling at his touch?

'I didn't have much time while I was studying, or during my intern year last year.' She had to pause to clear her throat. Her voice, husky at the best of times, had turned positively croaky since Jack had turned up. 'But this year I've been determined to *make* time for my drawing...sketching...painting.' She almost said more, but stopped herself in time. 'Everyone needs a relaxing hobby,' she asserted. 'An escape.'

Her father wouldn't agree. Charlotte would never have let any outside interests divert her from *her* goal. She'd been obsessed with her medical career, blinkered about it. Even her love for Jack had sprung from their work together.

As for Jack himself, he would be equally as focused, she suspected, now that he'd reached his current exalted heights. He might have jogged and swum and played tennis five years ago—to keep fit, he'd told her—but she doubted that he'd spare the time for such frivolities now that he was back in Australia, and heading for the very top. It was amazing enough that he was spending time here at the Art Gallery.

She broke eye contact at last. Lowering her gaze, she found her eyes riveted to Jack's casual shirt. Only she wasn't looking at the layer of fabric covering his chest, she was seeing—remembering—the power and the muscles and the strength *under* his shirt. Remembering the way Jack had looked on the beach in his brief swim-trunks, so virile and magnificent, his bare skin burnished a deep golden bronze…

She made a choking sound in her throat.

And promptly covered it up with a fit of coughing.

'Are you all right, Kate?' There was swift concern in Jack's voice, and she felt a tremor when she heard it. It was the same concern he'd shown for her after she'd nearly drowned…and while he was treating her black eye.

He's a master of polished charm, she reminded herself with a surge of scorn. He even managed to charm your hard-headed sister, remember. Until he tired of her.

The reminder of Charlotte was all she needed.

'I'm perfectly all right, thank you. I've had a bit of a cold, that's all.' It was the truth. She'd been a bit run down lately, with her long hours at the hospital, and the plans for the wedding, and a wave of pre-wedding jitters…

'Well, I'm glad you've kept on with your art, Kate,' Jack commented. 'I couldn't agree more…that everyone needs an escape, but…' He pursed his lips as if wondering whether to pursue the subject. 'I thought you *were* still studying? Aren't you intending to specialise?'

'Where did you get that idea?' Kate's tone was sharp.

His brow wrinkled. 'I know you said you weren't doing heart surgery, but I thought...' He paused, his eyes piercing hers. 'You're saying you're not specialising at all?'

Her chin rose a notch. 'That's right...I'm not. I'm sticking with general practice.' *We're not all as ambitious and as single-minded as you...and my father,* her eyes told him.

She expected to see a supercilious curl of his lip, a superior gleam in his eye, but his reaction was more of surprise than anything. He even looked faintly baffled.

'You didn't want to follow in your father's footsteps? Your sister's?' As he mentioned her sister the blue of his eyes turned flat under her gaze, hiding whatever emotion might have been there.

'I'd rather follow in my *mother's* footsteps,' she tossed back. 'She's a wonderful GP, and I want to be just like her.'

Not that she planned to work as a GP for long, but she needn't tell Jack that. She hadn't even told her parents yet that she'd decided to give up medicine once she started having children, as she and Brendan hoped to do in a year or so. Children needed their parents' time, as much as their love. In her spare time she would paint— it was something she could do in her own home—and hopefully, in time, she would be able to launch a successful career for herself as a portrait painter.

Brendan was the only one who knew of her secret plan, and, being a family-orientated man, he was fully supportive...as she was sure her mother would be too, once she was over the initial shock.

Her father was bound to throw up his hands in despair at the waste of all her long years of study, but he would have grandchildren to compensate. And she would always have her medical degree to fall back on, if necessary. Part-time locum work was always in demand.

'A GP like your mother...' Jack's eyes bored into her face for a long moment.

So now he realises I'm more like my mother than my father or sister, Kate thought wryly. I suppose he despises me now for having so little ambition.

Jack glanced at his watch. 'I must fly... I'm doing my teaching rounds in twenty minutes.' He paused. 'As soon as I can grab the time to visit Selwyn, I intend to go and congratulate him personally. When are your art lessons?'

She eyed him through narrowed, faintly startled eyes. Did he simply want to make sure he avoided coming during a class? Or did he want to avoid *her* in particular?

'One o'clock on Fridays,' she said, with a toss of her honey-gold curls. 'When I'm on day shift I go to an evening class.' As she'd be doing next week. 'Why do you ask?' she challenged him.

'No reason. Just curious.' He gave a quick grin as he turned and strode off. She stood a moment, staring after him, aware that she was shaking, trembling from head to toe.

She sighed in frustration. Why did Jack Savage affect her the way he did? A man she had every reason to loathe. A man who brought back painful memories of her sister. A man who was as emotionally remote, as insensitive, as focused on his exalted career as her father.

Or was he?

She swallowed, recalling Jack's reaction to her decision to go into general practice. He'd shown more surprise than disdain. And his statement about everyone needing a relaxing hobby had surprised *her*, coming from the lips of an ambitious, high-flying neurosurgeon.

As for his generous support for his friend, Selwyn Dodd, long before the artist became rich and famous, it showed he had a human, caring side and stood by his friends, even friends who could no nothing to further his career.

She frowned, and shook her head. She mustn't let a few unexpected human qualities blind her to the fact that Jack Savage had broken her sister's heart...that he accepted no responsibility for Charlotte's black despair.

She shivered, reluctantly recognising her own susceptibility to this powerfully attractive man. This *dangerously* attractive man. Her own hard-headed sister, she had to keep reminding herself, had fallen victim to that dangerous charm.

She might have become a victim herself if she hadn't had her sister's tragic experience to warn her...and if she hadn't had Brendan, her future husband, for protection.

Her lip trembled as she remembered that Brendan was going away tomorrow for his weekend in Melbourne. Some protection!

Not that she needed his *physical* protection. She smiled a little at the very thought. Simply knowing that in just over two weeks she would be Brendan's wife was protection enough. When she picked up her engagement ring from the jeweller's she would feel even safer.

As she turned to the next Archibald portrait, she shrugged off her foolish musings. It wasn't as if Jack Savage was pursuing her, for heaven's sake. If he'd shown the faintest sign of any *personal* interest in her, she would have told him about Brendan and her wedding at once. Naturally. But she hadn't had to. Jack didn't care about her, so there had been no need to. Any interest in her had died five years ago, when he'd found out that she was Charlotte's sister, and Chester Warren-Smith's daughter.

Just as her own feelings for him had vanished the moment she'd found out who *he* was.

It shouldn't be too difficult to avoid him in the days leading up to her wedding. A hard-working, highly in demand whirlwind like Dr Jack Savage. It was pure chance that she'd met him here today, in the few spare minutes he'd seized from his busy schedule to pop into the Gallery. She wasn't likely to bump into him again. It was even less likely that she'd find herself *alone* with him again.

So why was she even thinking about him?

CHAPTER SIX

SELWYN DODD held his art classes in an old converted warehouse in the Rocks, near the Sydney Harbour Bridge. His studio and living quarters were on the floor above. When Kate arrived at one o'clock on Friday, Selwyn was in a flurry, pacing about in a paint-smattered smock, his wild hair sticking out beneath a black cap.

'Ah, Kate...good. Now that we're all here we can get started.' His artistic hands fluttered in the exaggerated way he did everything. 'I'm afraid our usual male model had an accident on his way here and can't sit for us today. Luckily, an old friend of mine happened to be here when I took the call, and he's kindly agreed to fill in...on condition he remains incognito.'

Selwyn winked, enjoying their little subterfuge. 'He's a busy man and can only spare a short time, so let's get on with it, shall we?'

As Kate stepped over to her easel, Selwyn moved across to the raised platform where the stand-in male model was sitting with his back to the small class of five students, a black floor-length robe covering his nakedness. Kate hadn't noticed him until now, because his cloaked figure merged into the black velvet backdrop he was facing.

She felt a smile tug at her lips when she realised the man was wearing a fitted black balaclava over his head. For anonymity, obviously.

Selwyn whisked the black robe from his friend's

89

shoulders and drew him to his feet, positioning him so that he was standing with his back to the class. A murmur went up from the female students as the substitute model was revealed in all his naked glory.

He was magnificent...tall, spectacularly built, perfectly proportioned, with a warm golden tan that appeared to be his natural skin colour, his legs and arms a shade darker. He was standing with his head bowed and hands clasped loosely in front of his body, so that nothing detracted from the fluid, virile outline of his stunning frame. His powerful legs were slightly bent, one heel raised off the floor.

Kate felt her throat constrict as her gaze absorbed the superb lines, the taut muscles, the strong thighs. A heart-stopping memory stirred, bringing a prickling heat to her cheeks. That amazing physique...the six-foot plus height...the controlled power and strength.

Suddenly it looked so familiar...so blindingly, shockingly familiar. Only the depth of skin colour had changed...the burnt mahogany of five years ago having lightened to a gentler golden-bronze.

It wasn't possible!

A hysterical giggle rose to her throat. A serious-minded, highly respected neurosurgeon, posing in the nude in front of a class of art students? Worse, posing in front of someone he *knew*? Someone who'd already seen him half-naked in the past and just possibly might recognise him?

He wouldn't!

Would he?

She bit her lip. Perhaps he was hoping she *had* recognised him, so that he could enjoy her discomfort. Or mock it. Or was the balaclava to ensure that she *wouldn't* recognise him? It was five years since she'd sketched him at Shelly Beach. He'd hardly expect her to remember intimate details of his naked physique after all this time...

But she *did* remember. The more she looked, the more the mind-boggling suspicion grew. She'd sketched this smooth, well-muscled body before...seen it in her dreams...even fantasised about it for a time...much as she'd tried not to.

It *was* him. She'd be prepared to swear...

'Come on, Kate. Stop drooling and get to work. *Tempus fugit.*'

Her cheeks flamed as Selwyn tapped her on the shoulder. Shakily, she picked up a stick of charcoal and bent over her easel. But not before she'd caught the twinkle in Selwyn's eye.

Mortification swept through her. Had Jack Savage *told* Selwyn that he knew someone in the class? That they worked at the same hospital? Was that why Jack had insisted on wearing that balaclava? Not just for general anonymity, but to make sure that *she* in particular didn't recognise him?

But she *had* recognised him!

A slow, wicked smile curved her lips. If she felt so inclined, she could tease him about it later...threaten to show her sketches around the hospital...enjoying the joke at *his* expense. If she wanted to be really diabolical she could share the joke with her fellow residents.

Her impish smile widened...then faltered. Would Jack care, whatever she did? Would he be angry? Embarrassed? Or simply laugh it off? Did Jack Savage have a sense of humour? It might be interesting to find out.

But in the meantime she had to steady her hand sufficiently to earn her money's worth from today's art class!

As she flitted from one emergency patient to the next, Kate heaved a sigh. Her shift this evening was really dragging for some reason. She hadn't seen Jack Savage coming on duty at three, so hadn't had a chance to search his face for telltale signs of guilt or wariness. And any fun she might have derived from the incident had failed to eventuate because she'd decided against mentioning it to him or anyone else, not even her closest colleagues.

What if she'd been mistaken about Selwyn's stand-in model being Jack Savage? What if her memory had played tricks? There were plenty of spectacularly built males around. It didn't have to be him, simply because he was a friend of Selwyn Dodd's and had planned to visit Selwyn 'some time'.

But her main reason for not mentioning it—her main *worry*—was the growing fear that she might be becoming *obsessed* with Dr Jack Savage. Obsessed enough to imagine seeing him in places he'd never actually been. Obsessed enough to imagine him posing in the nude at her art class. Obsessed enough to keep on seeing his image in her mind—not just his breathtaking physique, but his face, his eyes, his gently taunting smile—when it was the last image in the world she wanted to see!

She didn't know whether to laugh or cry.

Five minutes later pandemonium broke out in the ER, and in the ensuing furore Jack Savage's image was swept from her mind. There'd been a street fight among some youths in the city, and two had been badly injured, cut by broken glass, while a third had a suspected broken arm. A group of their mates had brought them in, but just as Kate was about to examine one of the injured youths he started hurling abuse at one of the others, blaming him for starting the fight. The other lashed back at him with a clenched fist, just missing the youth's jaw.

As Kate and a nurse tried to drag them apart, the flying fist landed a vicious blow to the side of Kate's head, striking her just below the temple, near her eye.

She staggered back, half stunned. Other emergency staff came running to the rescue, and quickly brought the situation under control. While the other doctors and nurses on duty tended to the injured youths, the sister-in-charge insisted that Kate lie down on one of the trolleys.

'I'm all right,' Kate insisted groggily. 'I have to—'

'Lie *down*, doctor. You'll stay right there until Dr Lockwood's had a chance to examine you. You have bruises coming up already. And a black eye. A beauty.'

Kate groaned. A bride with a black eye...great! Would it fade by her wedding day? She closed her eyes. The room was still spinning.

When she opened them again a pair of wondrous blue eyes were swimming over her. Didn't Tony Lockwood have *brown* eyes? she wondered dazedly.

Her gaze gradually focused...then snapped wide. With a muffled yelp, she tried to jerk herself upright.

'Lie still! I want to take a look at you.' Strong hands were on her shoulders, holding her down. Gently but firmly.

'Dr Savage!' Kate croaked, making another attempt to wriggle upright. Without the slightest success. 'I don't need a *neurosurgeon*, for heaven's sake! I only have a black eye.'

'Indeed you have.' Something glimmered, deep in the blue eyes. As if they shared a secret. As if, Kate thought headily, he were remembering another black eye...at another time. One that *he'd* caused, while saving her life.

She swallowed, and lay still, the fight flowing out of her. She knew it would be futile to fight strength like his anyway...even if she wanted to. And she *didn't* want to, she realised. Suddenly she didn't have any fight left. Any *will* left. Maybe the blow had been more serious than she'd thought.

'Dr Lockwood asked me to take a look at you.' Jack was peering into her eyes. Clinically. Without expression. The total, dedicated doctor now. 'I was just leaving to go home,' he added conversationally, 'when I heard you'd been punched in the head by an irate patient. I popped in to find out how bad it was.'

He'd cared enough to come and check her out... She felt an odd little quiver inside. But of course... She promptly quenched the warm feeling. He would have checked out any of the hospital staff who'd suffered a bang to the head. Damaged heads were his specialty.

After his examination Jack called for a cold compress, put it in place with the same gentle, caring fingers that she remembered—despite trying not to—from five years ago, and ordered her not to move until he came back.

'But I'm on duty,' she argued, wondering what he meant by *coming back*. In a minute or two, did he mean, after he'd spoken to Dr Lockwood? Or was he going to stay a while longer, instead of going home as he'd intended?

She felt another flutter as she tried to sit up—only to

have him gently push her back again. 'It's a busy night,' she protested, annoyed that her voice was far huskier than normal. 'They *need* me. I'm fine now…truly. I'll put some ice on my eye when I get home.'

'You'll stay right there until I come back. I'll fill in for you until your relief comes on at midnight, which is only half an hour away. No arguments!' he rapped out as her lips parted.

She shut her mouth and lay back, aware that her heart was skittering…and fully aware that it had nothing to do with any delayed reaction to the bump on her head. It was purely a reaction to Jack Savage's amazing statement. The hospital's number two neurosurgeon, offering to fill in for a resident in the ER? It was unheard of. Specialists didn't fill in for residents. They didn't fill in for anybody. They swanned around doing only the important stuff.

But then, Jack Savage wasn't your usual god-like, unreachable specialist, she was beginning to realise. He noticed the people around him. He took pity on errant resident doctors who damaged his brand-new car. He helped out his friends when they were poor unknowns, struggling for recognition. He swallowed his pride to pose in the nude, risking being the butt of jokes, when an artist friend was in urgent need.

The *butt* of jokes… She felt a giggle rising at her unconscious pun. Jack would appreciate the joke, she fancied, almost wishing she could share it with him.

A sigh trembled from her lips. Brendan hated being the butt of jokes…

Brendan! Swallowing guiltily, she made an effort to conjure up her future husband's face. He seemed so far away at this moment. He *was* far away...out of reach in another state.

Brendan, why aren't you here? she wondered miserably. *You* should be here comforting me, not Jack Savage.

Least of all Jack Savage.

She must have fallen asleep, because the next thing she knew, someone was lifting her from the hospital trolley.

'What—?' Opening her eyes, she saw Jack's face above her, disturbingly close. *'What are you doing?'* she gasped out, realising that the powerful arms holding her were *Jack's* arms...that the glinting blue eyes smiling into hers were *Jack's* eyes.

This was Dr Jack Savage, the hospital's high-powered neurosurgeon, carrying her through the ER in his arms, in full view of staff and patients!

'I'm taking you to my car and driving you home,' Jack said calmly. 'And then I'll be putting you to bed.'

Putting her to bed?

'D-don't be silly.' Alarm raced through her. 'I—I'm awake now. I can drive myself. My car's outside!' It was a ragged cry. 'L-let me down!'

'You're not fit to walk and you're not fit to drive.' Jack kept right on walking, striding out into the night. 'The staff agree with me.'

'You've been *discussing* me?' She resorted to anger. Anything to cover the frantic fluttering inside her. 'If you won't let me drive, I'll sleep in the doctors' lounge tonight. *Let me down!*'

'No way. You have the day off tomorrow, I'm told, and you'll spend it resting at home. Doctor's orders.'

'This is ridiculous!' she burst out, but he only held

her closer, crushed up against his chest. 'I—I'm fine,' she mumbled, but her words were muffled against his shirt.

'You had a nasty blow to the head. A clenched fist, I'm told. There's no sign of concussion, but you were badly shaken. And you have a shocker of a black eye.' He was striding across the car park now, heading for *his* car, not hers.

'I can't leave my car here all night!' she wailed.

'It'll be perfectly safe. You can pick it up tomorrow. Or Sunday. I'm sure your flatmate will drive you back to the hospital,' he said as they reached his shiny BMW. He lowered her gently to the ground, but still didn't let her go, supporting her until he'd unlocked his car and had gently eased her into the passenger seat.

Kate swallowed as she settled into the soft plush leather. Melanie had gone away for the weekend, to stay with her parents in the Blue Mountains. *Brendan was away too*. Should she tell Jack that she was alone for the weekend...or not?

No! Her heart quailed at the very thought. Best not. Let him think that her flatmate was at home, in bed. Let him go on wondering if her flatmate was a male or a female. With both Melanie and Brendan away, she felt far too vulnerable. Which was stupid, she knew. That punch must have left her weaker than she'd thought.

She tilted her head back and closed her eyes, only speaking when Jack asked for directions. He didn't ask any further questions, or bother with small talk. The man was probably as anxious to drop her off home and be on his way as she was to see the last of *him*...

She allowed herself to relax a trifle...even though she could still feel the warm imprint of his hands on her waist, his fingers clasping her legs...still feel his heart-beat against her cheek...still feel the tender, capable touch of his fingers on her skin as he'd examined her bruised face.

Firm, gentle hands... A deep sigh quivered through her.

'Nearly there, Kate.'

She could have wept at the gentle compassion in his voice. This was *Jack*...the Jack she'd first known. The Jack who'd saved her from the sea...who'd cared for her afterwards...

But he *wasn't* Jack. She stirred restlessly in her seat. This was Jonathan Savage. Heartless, insensitive Jonathan Savage, who'd never shown an iota of compassion for the woman who'd loved him, the woman he'd walked out on, the woman who'd died. Her sister!

And even if he had...even if he'd been the most loving, compassionate man in the world...what would it matter now? In two weeks' time she was marrying another man!

Oh, Brendan, I wish you were here! The silent, frantic cry rose from deep within her. The man she'd promised to marry *was* loving and compassionate, in his own quiet, reserved way. And she did love him. She could name a dozen reasons why she loved him.

Jack's voice made her jump. Her eyes flicked open.

'Here's number seven...is this it?'' he asked, pulling into the kerb outside the narrow-fronted Paddington terrace house she shared with Melanie. It belonged to Kate's father, but she'd only moved in on condition that they both paid rent. 'There aren't any lights on,' he commented.

'No...well, it's late,' she mumbled, intimating that her

flatmate would have already gone to bed. 'Thank you, Dr Savage.' *Keep it formal.*

She was talking to fresh air. He'd already left the driver's seat and was striding round to help her out. From there he insisted on escorting her to her door. And once she'd unlocked it he brushed aside her protests and ushered her inside, his hand at her elbow.

Silence swirled around them as she snapped on the hall lights.

'Well, thank—'

'There's a note for you,' Jack told her. It was propped up against a vase on the umbrella stand. The writing on it was large and clear. 'ENJOY YOUR WEEKEND. BACK MONDAY MORNING. LOVE MEL.' Jack turned to face her, his eyes speculative, searching hers. 'Mel's your flatmate?'

She made a supreme effort to stay calm, not to flush, somehow managing to answer airily, with a shrug. 'She's gone home for the weekend. It's her mother's birthday.'

'So there's no one else here?'

The skin at her nape tingled. 'I'm a big girl now,' she quipped. *Why didn't he go?*

'Where's your bedroom?'

Now she did flush, her face flaming. 'My...*what*?'

His mouth curved in a wry smile. 'It's your doctor asking, not a serial rapist. I want you to go upstairs, Kate, get undressed, and get into bed. I'll make you a cup of tea. You do drink tea? Or would you prefer coffee? Or hot milk?'

She could feel herself trembling, sweat prickling her upper lip. It was stupid. He was just showing the concern that any doctor who'd driven her home would show to a colleague who'd suffered a bang to the head.

'I—I can get myself a cup of tea,' she stammered. 'And I—I'm not ready to go to bed…'

'Don't argue. I'm not leaving until I've made sure you're all right and settled down for the night. I'll prepare a cold compress while you're getting undressed. A bit more ice treatment won't go amiss. The kitchen's down there, I take it?' He waved a hand.

She sighed. 'End of the passage, through the dining room.' She jutted her chin. 'I'll lie on the sofa…in here.' She reached out to flick on the lounge room lights. 'I'll go to bed after I've had my tea.' *After you've gone*, her eyes told him. 'It's only a black eye, for heaven's sake.'

'You're one stubborn woman.'

And he was one masterful man. But she wasn't about to tell him that. She felt too starkly alone and exposed, here in her silent, empty house with him. If only she'd picked up her engagement ring today, so she could have waved it at him! It was ready, but she hadn't had a chance yet to pick it up from the jeweller's.

Never mind. The moment Jack came back from the kitchen she would tell him about Brendan. Just knowing that Jack was aware of her coming wedding day would be enough to fortify her.

She gave an exasperated sigh as she kicked off her shoes and sank down on the sofa, swinging her feet up onto the cushions. Why should she *need* fortifying? she brooded. This was *Jack Savage*, the man who'd callously hurt her sister. The man she'd vowed always to hate.

A lump rose to her throat, her eyes clouding. But she *didn't* hate him. That was the whole trouble. He was nothing like the Jonathan Savage her father had long reviled. Nothing like the heartless, insensitive Jonathan Savage she'd always expected him to be. Not at all the kind of man she'd imagined a highly ambitious neurosurgeon would be.

More and more he was like the Jack she'd once known and had felt so instantly drawn to, so mysteriously connected to. The Jack who'd been so caring, so strong, and yet so gentle.

She shook her head to clear it. *Think of Charlotte.* Jack had shown no compassion towards her sister. None. That was what she must always keep in mind.

She could hear him clattering about in the kitchen. This was crazy! She drew in a tremulous breath. He was making a fuss about nothing. Other than a slight ache around her eye, she felt fine.

'Can you find everything?' she yelled out to him, fully prepared to jump up again to help him out. The sooner she was rid of him the better.

'No problem.' The answer was immediate. 'Stay where you are!'

She dropped her head back on the cushions and closed her eyes. *So caring, so strong, yet so gentle...* Who was the real Jack Savage? she wondered. The Jack she was seeing now? Or the unfeeling Jonathan that Charlotte had known? Another sigh whispered from her.

'Here we are.' He came in bearing a tray. It held two mugs of hot water with teabags in them, a sugar bowl, a small jug of milk, a packet of frozen peas and a teatowel.

He set the tray down on her small coffee table and proceeded to wrap the frozen peas in the teatowel. 'Hold this against your eye,' he commanded as he handed it to her. 'Now...milk? Sugar?'

She shook her head. 'Black will be fine,' she said faintly, pressing the makeshift ice-pack to her face. 'Thanks.' She gulped. 'It looks pretty bad, does it?'

He raised an eyebrow as he removed the teabag from her mug and dropped it on the tray. 'You haven't looked?' He smiled and shook his head. 'Most women would have demanded a mirror long ago. It *is* pretty bad, but don't worry, you're still beautiful.'

As she gulped in another breath, ready to fling back a desperate retort about a bride needing to be at her best for her wedding day, so that he'd *know*, Jack asked solicitously, moving the coffee table closer to her elbow, 'Can you reach it from there? Good.'

And then, to her horror, he lowered himself down on the sofa *she* was on, perching himself on the edge, facing her, his thighs a solid warmth against her stockinged legs, his knees touching the small coffee table. She lost her voice completely.

'Now...tell me. How did your art class go?' Jack asked conversationally.

The question caught her by surprise. Her gaze flew to his. The second their eyes met...the second she saw the glimmer in the piercing blue...she *knew*.

'It *was* you!' It was a husky yelp. She felt a rush of fire to her cheeks, mortification flooding through her the second the words were out. She buried her heated face in the ice-pack, mentally kicking herself. If she'd pretended ignorance she could have saved herself this appalling embarrassment. She'd admitted that she'd known it was him, that she'd *recognised* him! *He* would never have told her.

Would he?

'You recognised me? After all this time?' A slow smile stretched his lips, adding creases to his cheeks and around his eyes. 'Well, well, well.'

She found it hard to meet him in the eye. He was amused, damn him, not the least bit embarrassed himself! And, even worse, he hadn't forgotten the near-naked sketch she'd done of him five years ago. She cast around for a line of attack.

Inspiration came.

'So...you're admitting you posed in the nude in front of a roomful of art students? An eminent, respected neurosurgeon, flaunting his naked body in front of strangers!'

His smile turned sardonic, a warning gleam in his eye now. 'I'm not admitting to anything...if you're thinking of spreading lurid tales about me...or showing your artwork around the hospital. Not that anyone would believe you... *"An eminent, respected neurosurgeon"*,' he mimicked, *' "flaunting his naked body in front of strangers!"'* He gave a soft laugh. 'They'd think you were off your rocker.'

Would they? She thought of Georgia...and Ella...and quite a few others who'd mentally undressed him many a time.

'Don't worry, you're safe,' she assured him unsteadily. 'I've no intention of revealing your lurid secret. You went to enough lengths to hide your identity.' Now it was her own eyes that were shimmering. 'I won't breathe a word. Unless you drive me to it...by spreading lurid stories about *me*...' That she was a sex-crazed amateur artist, forever sketching nude males!

'Stories about *you*, Dr Smith? Now why in the world

would I want to do that?' He raised his mug to his lips, his eyes dancing over the rim.

No…why would he bother? she reflected ruefully. It would be beneath an exalted neurosurgeon to spread gossip about a mere resident. With an impatient gesture, she discarded the ice-pack and concentrated on her tea.

'I'm curious, Kate…' Jack's voice was a silken purr. 'Did you recognise me with an artist's eye…or a *woman's*?'

She nearly spilt her tea. Flustered, she gripped the handle of her mug for dear life, fixing her gaze on the swirling contents. Anything to avoid looking at *him*. 'P-purely as an artist,' she assured him shakily.

'Are you sure, Kate?' His voice was low and seductive now, his face suddenly far too close, his eyes catching hers, holding her startled gaze for a heady second. 'But I'm embarrassing you…' He gave a soft chuckle and sat back, allowing her to breathe again.

'You know,' he added musingly, 'you're not at all how I imagined Kate Warren-Smith would be. But you prefer Kate Smith, don't you? And that's a part of it. You want to follow your own star, be yourself, not a shadow of your father…or your sister. Not that you ever would be. You're a different type of person altogether.'

Kate stirred uneasily. Was that a criticism…or a compliment? Her father was a brilliant surgeon, who'd reached the very top of his field with single-minded purpose and cold-hearted dedication, and her sister had vowed to be just like him. Was that what Jack meant? There was nothing brilliant or fanatically ambitious about Kate.

'You care *for* people…the whole person, not just for what ails them,' Jack said. 'I've seen you at work...heard my colleagues comment on what a caring doctor you are.' He pursed his lips. 'You must take after your mother. She's a GP, you said? Like you want to be?'

Kate nodded, lifting her chin higher. 'I'd be very happy to be like my mother. She's a wonderful person. Warm and caring and compassionate.' She sighed, gazing into the dregs of her tea. 'She'd forgive anyone anything.' Even her father's heartless neglect over the years. And her mother was still considering his needs before her own, still consoling him for the loss of his beloved elder daughter.

Did her father appreciate his wife's loving devotion to him? she wondered wistfully. The only real emotion her father had ever shown in Kate's presence was when Charlotte had died.

A shadow flitted across her face. Charlotte's death might have brought her parents back together, but it had driven Jack and herself apart. It would always keep them apart. Even if there were no Brendan.

'I wish things could have been different, Kate,' Jack murmured.

Her head jerked up, her eyes widening. He was leaning close to her again, very close, his great shoulders seeming to swamp her, envelop her, reminding her suddenly—scorchingly—of how she'd once felt, cradled against them. Safe, protected, nurtured...every nerve-end alive...

She twitched back as if stung.

'What do you mean?' It was a ragged whisper. And an unwise question, she realised too late.

She saw his chest rise and fall before he answered

with a question of his own. 'Will your sister always be between us, Kate?'

Her mouth went dry. Before she realised what was happening, he'd plucked the mug from her fingers, set it down on the table with his, and, pushing it aside, shifted closer so that he could take hold of her arms. She felt the warmth of his fingers heating her skin through the sleeves of her shirt, felt his eyes burning into hers.

'Jack—' Her voice was a pathetic croak. His touch, his searing gaze, were paralysing her, mesmerising her, turning her bones to tingling fire.

'Hush, Kate... I want to say something.'

She found her eyes riveted to his mouth, helplessly fascinated to hear what he might be going to say next— even though her head was telling her she mustn't listen.

'There was a time, Kate...before you knew who I was...before I knew who you were...when I kissed you and the world tilted on its axis.' The compelling gaze held hers. 'Do you think that could ever happen again, Kate? Could you and I ever go back to the way we were...to the golden mermaid and the unknown man who plucked her from the sea? And start all over again?'

Before she could answer or utter a protest—or even react—his mouth was on hers, gently seeking an answer.

The melting warmth of his lips, the delicious sensations that swept through her the moment they touched hers, dissolved any fight in her, scattering all common sense and blotting out everything but the two of them. Hot desire raced through her, her body melting into his, a moan slipping from deep within her as she trembled against his rock-hard strength, his burning warmth.

She felt weak and dizzy, helpless to control her arms as they wound themselves round his neck, helpless to stop her fingers clutching at his head, sliding through his hair, helpless to stop the raging tide of passion that was threatening to swamp her.

She'd only ever felt like this once before…this devastating weakness, this blinding passion, this piercing, head-spinning ecstasy…and only ever with him…

'You do still feel it, don't you, Kate?' Jack murmured against her lips. 'There is still hope for us…if we can only let go of the past.'

Hope for us? She gave a muffled cry as sanity rushed back.

'Oh, Jack…' She let her hands slide from his shoulders, shaking her head, aware of a scorching pain deep inside. Her body was still trembling, still quivering with sensations she knew she would have to quench, and quickly…and then forget for all time. 'I hope we *can* be friends, but—' Her voice cracked. 'I shouldn't have let you kiss me, Jack. I—I don't know why I did. I…it didn't mean that I…'

She let her voice trail off, looking up at him with stricken eyes.

'Jack…I'm getting married in two weeks!'

CHAPTER SEVEN

THE look of shocked disbelief on Jack's face almost made her cry out. In an instinctive movement she reached out to him, then froze, letting her hand drop, realising it was a mistake.

He snatched up her left hand. 'I can't see a ring,' he rasped. A sudden fierce gleam intensified the sharp blue of his eyes. 'You wouldn't be kidding me, would you? Just to—' He bit off what he'd been about to say, but he might just as well have said it. *To keep me at arms' length.*

She shook her head, his reaction shaking her. Or was it just wounded pride he felt? She'd allowed him to kiss her. An engaged woman, about to be married. Did he feel she'd made a fool of him?

She'd made more of a fool of herself!

She pulled her hand free, curling it into a white-knuckled fist. 'It's true, Jack,' she choked out. 'My—my ring's at the jeweller's being altered. I meant to pick it up today, but I...I forgot.' Would he see her as fast and cheap now? As disloyal and untrustworthy? A sharp pang knifed through her.

A derisive eyebrow shot up at the admission, *'I forgot.'* Already a veil had come down over his eyes, wiping out the naked emotion he'd revealed for a second...making her wonder if it had ever been there to see.

'Do you forget your fiancé as easily as you forget his ring?' His voice was harsh, heavy with sarcasm.

Heat flamed along her cheekbones. 'Jack, I'm sorry,' she whispered. 'I just—I just wanted us to be friends again.' Would that explain her appalling weakness? Her loss of control?

His mouth twisted, as if he were thinking how impossible that was...now. 'So who's the lucky man?' he asked roughly. 'A hotshot heart specialist like your father? Or a caring GP, perhaps...like your mother? Like you say you want to be?'

'He's not a doctor...I'd never marry a doctor,' Kate stated flatly, and saw his brow rise even higher.

She caught a spark of something in his eyes and wondered what it was. Surprise? Derision? Disbelief?

'Well, I'm sure it's someone your parents approve of.' His tone was ice-cold, cynical, intimating that they would never have approved of him...the man who'd broken the heart of one daughter and might well have done the same to her younger sister if she'd been foolish enough to get involved with him.

Which she might well have been tempted to do, Kate acknowledged shakily, if she hadn't been safely engaged to be married...and if she could have forgotten how deeply Jack had hurt her sister seven years ago—intentionally or not—and overlooked his callous disregard for Charlotte.

'So...you're getting married.' Still the same scathing, flaying tone. 'Funny you never thought to mention it before. Just as well you remembered when you did.'

Before he made a complete fool of himself, did he mean?

'I try to keep my work and my private life separate,'

she mumbled, knowing it was a lame excuse for not telling him earlier. It was a wonder no one in the ER had suggested calling Brendan tonight, she thought, when she'd been almost knocked out. But why should they have? It had been a busy night and they could see she was in good hands.

Good, safe hands… She shivered.

'Well, you're not at work now,' Jack pointed out dryly. 'So tell me. If he's not a doctor, what is he? A barrister? A wealthy stockbroker? A high-flying business tycoon?'

Her eyes snapped with contempt. How little he knew her after all! 'He's an accountant.' She tilted her chin. 'A *tax* accountant.' A home-loving man, she thought with a tinge of the old bitterness. A dedicated family man, who'd be more devoted to his wife and children than any doctor would be, with his precious all-consuming career absorbing his time and his attention…and the bulk of his love.

'Ah.' Jack nodded sagely, his eyes still cold. 'The family accountant, is he? I bet he's a top-of-the-tree tax whiz, *au fait* with all the legal loopholes in the book. A paragon in every way.'

'He's nothing to do with my family,' Kate snapped, glaring at him. Why was Jack always so harsh and bitter towards her family, when *he* was the one deserving condemnation? A fact that she'd be wise to keep in mind in future!

'He has his own business,' she hissed. 'A small office in the suburbs.'

Jack drew in his lips. 'Is that how you met him? Getting tax advice from him?'

'No, it wasn't.' She jutted her chin. 'I met him at St

Mark's, when I was in Orthopaedics. He'd broken his leg in a car accident. He was in hospital for several weeks.' He would have recovered much quicker, the wayward thought occurred to her, if he'd had Jack Savage's strength and fitness.

'You fell for a patient?'

'No!' She flushed. 'I mean—' She stopped, and started again. 'We became *friends* while he was in hospital…that's all. We found that we both shared a common passion…' now why did she have to use *that* word? '…and it led to him asking me out. *After* he'd recovered and gone home.'

'A common *passion*…' Jack seized on the word. 'You mean for each other?' His eyes glinted, but without humour.

'A common *interest*,' she corrected, more sharply than she'd intended.

'In…?' Jack pursed his lips. 'Art?' he hazarded. 'A shared appreciation of the naked form? A burning desire to paint each other in the nude?' His eyes mocked her.

Heat surged into her cheeks. Did he have to keep harping on nudity? 'Brendan's not artistic,' she said tersely. She'd never even seen Brendan in the nude! Not even at the hospital.

'Ah. Then perhaps…a shared passion for swimming?' A dark eyebrow shot up. 'Sunbaking? Frolicking on the beach?'

'Brendan hates the beach. He's fair-skinned and burns easily. Jack—'

'No, don't spoil my fun.' *Fun*, she thought shakily. Is that what this is?

'Let me see…' Jack tapped his jaw with a fingertip. 'You both like driving fast cars? Speeding about in enclosed spaces…particularly in car parks?' There was a real glitter in the blue eyes now, his sense of humour stirring despite himself, melting the chilling coldness.

Speeding? Brendan was the most sedate driver in the world. 'You're making fun of me,' she breathed unsteadily.

'I like a bit of fun. Don't you have fun with…what's his name?'

'Brendan.' She couldn't look Jack in the eye. She was afraid she might catch the laughter in his eyes and be tempted to respond to it.

Did she have fun with Brendan? They smiled together…they even laughed together…sometimes…but *fun?* For no particular reason? She couldn't imagine Brendan having a conversation like Jack was having now, just for the sheer fun of it—even if the fun was tinged with mockery. Brendan didn't indulge in meaningless, light-hearted banter. He was the sensible, serious type.

But she mustn't compare them. They were two completely different men. Not just physically. She swallowed. Physically they were as different as…David and Goliath. Yet puny little David, she rallied, had won over the mighty Goliath. And average-sized Brendan was far superior to Jack Savage in every way that mattered. He was rock-solid and dependable. Steadfast and undemanding. A thoroughly nice, gentle, easy-going guy.

Jack was…

Jack was *Jonathan Savage.*

She let her eyes chill under his gaze. 'Have you finished your little game?' she asked coolly. 'Let me put you out of your misery. You're never going to guess. We discovered we're both Gilbert and Sullivan fans!'

Jack threw back his head and laughed. '*The Mikado*? *The Pirates of Penzance*? Well...you're right, I never would have guessed.' His eyes gleamed. 'You both sang "Three Little Maids from School" together, did you, while you were checking his pulse?'

He broke into a deep baritone, singing the entire song from memory.

Kate blinked, wondering what on earth Jack was going to reveal about himself next. She tried to imagine Brendan spontaneously breaking into song, and couldn't. He'd be far too self-conscious...even if he had the voice for it, or could sing in tune.

'No, we didn't sing together,' she admitted, aware of a faint stab of regret. She was tempted to reel off a few bars herself, from one of the famous patter songs. *She* knew all the words too. 'We just enjoy going to the shows during the season. We enjoy the songs. The music. It's fun.' She wanted Jack to know that they did have some fun together.

'Good for you.' The shimmer of amusement in Jack's eyes died. 'So...you share a passion for Gilbert and Sullivan.' He paused, his eyes taking on a quite different glitter. 'And for each other...I hope? Where *is* your fiancé, by the way? He's not staying with you while your flatmate's away?'

Kate felt heat flash along her cheekbones. She flicked her tongue over lips that had gone deplorably dry. 'No, he's not,' she said shortly.

Would Brendan have stayed here with her if he'd been in town? Most likely not. He had old-fashioned ideas of morality. It was why he'd proposed so soon after they'd started going out together, and why he'd pressed her for a wedding date the moment he had his ring on her finger.

He'd wanted to legalise their relationship as quickly as possible. No sex before marriage for Brendan. Kisses, cuddles, and some cautious petting were all he'd allow. If the petting threatened to get out of control, he'd call an immediate halt and hastily—reluctantly—remove himself from her presence.

'I thought you were anxious to get home.' She shifted restlessly. 'Jack, I'm fine now, and I—I'd like to go to bed.'

He raised an eyebrow and she flushed again. Flustered, she gave him a push. Why could she never mention the word 'bed' in Jack's presence without feeling hot all over? She was furious with herself for reacting to him…reacting to that mocking eyebrow.

It was just nervous tension! Because she was home alone for the weekend and Jack was here with her, making her feel doubly alone. Alone and vulnerable. She had to get Jack out of the house before he found out that Brendan had gone away for the weekend!

'Yes, I must let you…go to bed,' Jack murmured, rising to his feet at last.

She let her breath out as he stepped back, giving her some breathing space. When he was at a safe distance, she swung her legs to the floor and stood up herself. Far too quickly. It was a big mistake. She felt her head spinning. As she swayed, she felt Jack's hand, in a lightning movement, clamp round her arm.

'I'm all right,' she gasped. 'I stood up too quickly.'

'You're not all right,' Jack grated. 'I'm taking you up to your bedroom, and this time there'll be no arguments.'

It was his doctor's voice. Coldly professional, implacable. The voice of a man who didn't intend to take no for an answer, no matter how forcibly she might say it. There'd be no fobbing him off this time.

'And just to make sure you don't argue...' Before she could blink, let alone protest, Jack swung her up in his arms, just as he had earlier, at the hospital. Only this time there was steely purpose in his face, and pure steel in his arms. This time she knew he meant business. She bowed to the inevitable and remained still in his arms. It was the easiest way out. The quickest way out.

But she didn't relax. Every nerve-end remained screamingly on edge as he carefully manoeuvred her up the narrow staircase to her room.

Before he released her onto her bed, he looked down at her for a moment with a crooked smile. 'You're still aware of me, aren't you, Kate? Despite your sister. Despite your father. Despite your fiancé...and your wedding day in a couple of weeks.'

Her breath seized in her throat. She unlocked her voice with an effort. 'You—that's crazy!' she breathed. 'Let me go!' She began to struggle, her eyes wild, panicky, her heart crashing against her ribs. 'Let me go or I'll scream. I'll call the police. I—I'll have you struck off!'

His eyes narrowed, but the wry smile remained. 'For putting you safely to bed? You've nothing to fear from me, Kate, and you know it.' He lowered her down as he spoke, her flailing arms making no impression on him. 'Only from yourself.'

She gaped speechlessly up at him·as he slid his hands free and stepped back. As he straightened he stood looking down at her, his eyes taunting her. 'Have you told your father I'm back? Have you told your fiancé? Did you tell Brendan we met five years ago? That we're now working together?'

She gathered all her strength to answer without croaking, without flinching. 'None of my family ever mention Jonathan Savage,' she scraped out, scowling for good measure as she said it. 'And my father's been away for most of the week...at a seminar in Hong Kong.'

'No...I didn't think you had.' He laughed softly. A wolfish laugh, with a cynical edge. 'But is that the only reason you haven't mentioned me to your future husband, Kate?' He let that sink in for a second.

The silence in the room pulsed around her, the second seeming like an endless, screaming minute.

'I'm not Jonathan Savage any more, remember...' His voice cut through the tense silence. 'Certainly not the Jonathan Savage your family were so sure they knew.' His voice hardened as he bit the words out. 'I'm Dr Jack Savage now, and I'm assistant neurosurgeon at St Mark's hospital. *Your* hospital. Get used to the idea, Kate. I'm back, and I'm here to stay.'

'Well, keep away from *me*!' It was a ragged plea.

Jack spread his hands, then asked softly, with a sigh, 'Why do I disturb you so much, Kate?' His eyes glittered. 'Why were you so afraid to let me carry you up to your bedroom...a fellow doctor, simply wanting to make sure you're all right after you nearly lost your balance? Why do you jump every time I touch you? Why did you respond when I kissed you?'

He waved a dismissive hand as panicked eyes flew to his, as her mouth flew open to snap out a denial. 'OK, OK, so you were in a weakened state. You didn't mean it. You were just responding—mindlessly—to a phantom memory from the past. You were just missing your fiancé. OK.'

He backed away at last, a taunting smile on his lips. 'Let's leave it at that, shall we? Sleep well, Kate...I'll see myself out.'

He strode from the room, and within minutes she heard the front door slam shut.

She flopped back onto the pillows. Sleep well? How could she sleep well after all that!

She didn't. For hour after hour she thrashed about in her bed, getting tangled in the sheets, getting hotter and more desperate until finally, just as the birds started warbling in the trees, she fell into a deep, exhausted sleep.

She slept until late Saturday morning, then reluctantly dragged herself out of bed. Her eye still felt tender when she touched it, and the bruising above and below was a sight, but she had no headache, no real pain. Only a strange *heart*ache.

She was missing Brendan, that was all it was. Being on her own for the weekend, without him, without even Melanie. She wished he'd call her, if only to say hi! It would give her a chance to tell him how much she was missing him, and how much she loved him. She wanted to hear *him* say how much he loved *her*.

Not that she was expecting him to call. Brendan knew that she'd worked late last night and would want to sleep in late this morning, being her day off. And by now—she glanced at her watch—he'd be at his stamp exhibition, his mind immersed in his beloved stamps.

After a healthy breakfast of fresh fruit, yoghurt, toast and coffee she had a long leisurely bath, then pulled on jeans and a scoop-necked top. She threw an oversized shirt over the top—one of her father's discards that she used as a painting smock. She'd work for a couple of hours, she decided, before heading off to her mother's, popping into the jeweller's on the way.

It was warm enough today to go for a swim in her parents' pool. She sighed. A leisurely swim sounded far more enticing than working on seating arrangements.

She headed for the small spare room that she used as a studio, and unveiled the portrait she was painting. It was a head and shoulder portrait of Melanie. Mel had sat for her in their spare moments together, and the portrait only needed a couple of finishing touches before it was ready to be framed, then given to Melanie as her bridesmaid's gift.

As she was dabbing on the final stroke, the doorbell rang.

She froze, her paintbrush poised in mid air. No…it couldn't be *him*. She'd made it clear—embarrassingly clear, she realised with a rush of heat—that she didn't want him anywhere near her. In the harsh light of day, her hysterical reaction to him last night was nothing less than *mortifying*.

No…it was more likely her mother. Or her father. But they were expecting her to spend the afternoon and evening at their place, so why would *they* be calling round to see her?

It must be someone collecting for charity. Or a door-to-door salesman.

She grabbed her purse and headed for the front door.

Her eyes snapped wide in shock as she pulled it open. It *was* him. A quite different Dr Jack Savage from last night. A sporty Jack Savage in navy-edged white tennis gear, his casual top stretched tight across his broad chest, showing off the stunning width of his shoulders, his shorts revealing the athletic power of his strong tanned legs.

The same legs she'd studied so carefully and reproduced so graphically in her art class yesterday.

'D-Dr Savage,' she said faintly. *Keep it impersonal,* she thought. *And don't apologise for last night...don't even mention it.* Somehow, in sporty tennis gear, obviously on his way to a game, Jack didn't seem quite so threatening. Despite the powerful bare legs.

'Just passing by on my way back from tennis,' Jack said easily.

On his way *back*? She gulped. He'd already played! He didn't even look sweaty, let alone show the faintest sign of fatigue.

'Did—did you win?' she heard herself stammering inanely.

'Won three sets, lost two.' A satisfied smile. 'Tight match...could have gone either way.'

He'd played five sets? 'Congratulations,' she said faintly. Was there no end to Jack Savage's talents? No end to his boundless energy?

'Thought I'd call in and see how you are,' Jack said. 'That punch knocked you about a bit. No wonder you were a bit fraught last night. Perfectly understandable.'

Was he making excuses for her? Or was this a smoothly veiled apology for the provocative remarks he'd made last night? Either way, she grabbed at it.

'Yes...I, er, wasn't myself last night. But I'm perfectly normal now. See?' She waved a hand over her paint-smeared shirt. 'I've been working.'

'Your fiancé's not here, holding your hand? Stroking your brow?'

She felt her skin heating. 'I—I haven't been up long. I slept in. And later this afternoon,' she rushed on, 'we'll be working on the guest seating for the wedding. At my mother's.' She hoped that Jack would assume *'we'll be working'* included Brendan.

'Ah…then you won't mind if I just take a look at that injury of yours…to make sure all's well?'

As he made a move to step inside, her phone started ringing. She glanced up at Jack. 'I told you, I'm—'

'Go and answer it.' He waved a hand. 'I'll wait…'

She bit her lip, then turned and dashed back into the house, realising as she snatched up the phone from the passage wall that Jack had stepped in after her and was pulling the front door shut behind him.

CHAPTER EIGHT

SHE heard the pips of a mobile phone. 'Hullo,' she croaked, turning her back on Jack so he couldn't see the colour rising to her cheeks. So much for feeling calm and normal again!

'Kate? Is that you?'

It was *Brendan's* voice!

'Darling!' she cried. 'It's wonderful to hear from you!' As she gushed out her eager greeting for Jack's benefit, she realised she was overdoing it. She lowered her voice, hoping Jack wouldn't have guessed by now that Brendan was away. 'How's it going? Where are you?'

'I'm ringing from the exhibition building. We're just taking a break. It's all going well. Marvellously,' he enthused. 'How are *you*?' he asked, as if something in her voice had just penetrated. 'You sound a bit...I don't know. A bit odd. Different.'

He chose *now* to be telepathic!

'No, no, I'm fine.' She was about to add, *I'm missing you*, but she didn't want Jack to hear and know for certain that her fiancé was away. She tried to explain away her fevered greeting. 'A patient gave me a black eye last night, that's all. I look a bit of a sight.'

'Oh, no. Will it be better by the wedding?' Brendan asked anxiously.

He sounded more concerned about how she looked, Kate thought tremulously, than how she might be feeling. She shook off the fractious thought. She'd already told him she was fine. So what did she expect from him…a flood of sympathy?

'I'm sure it will,' she said, hoping she was right. 'If it's not, a bit of make-up will hide it.'

'Well, I hope so. I'd better go, darling. I just wanted to let you know that I won't be flying home Sunday night as planned. I'll be staying here overnight and leaving first thing Monday morning. The other judges want to get together over dinner tomorrow night, for a postmortem after the exhibition. They've asked me to join them. You don't mind, do you? I wasn't going to see you until Monday night anyway.'

She felt a faint twinge that he hadn't rung simply to say hullo, or because he was missing her. He'd only rung to tell her he'd be staying another night in Melbourne.

'Of course I don't mind. Enjoy the extra night,' she added lightly—then could have kicked herself as she remembered that Jack was undoubtedly listening to every word. 'I love you,' she breathed into the phone.

'Me too. Must fly. Bye!'

She heaved a faint sigh as she hung up. He hadn't even told her he was missing her! Of course, he'd be reticent about saying a thing like that over the phone, when others could be listening in. And he'd only been gone for one night so far, for heaven's sake!

And now he'd be away for two more. Not just tonight, as she'd expected, but tomorrow night as well.

Well, so what? She straightened her shoulders before turning back to Jack. She was making a mountain out of a molehill. What was one weekend apart?

If she'd freaked out for a second, it was all Jack Savage's fault!

Well, she was back to normal again, and Jack couldn't affect her any more. It was just that punch to her head that had made her a bit fragile and fraught last night. And Brendan being away.

'Your fiancé, I presume?' Jack's voice was velvet-smooth. 'You won't be seeing him today after all? Or…tonight?' he added silkily.

She looked him square in the eye. Why not tell him, straight out, that Brendan was away? What was she afraid of? Jack had accused her last night of being afraid of her own feelings. Well, she wasn't! And she'd jolly well show him she wasn't.

'Brendan's at a stamp fair in Melbourne,' she told him with amazing steadiness. 'He was just calling to say hi.' No need to tell Jack that he wasn't coming back until Monday.

'A *stamp* fair?' Amusement flickered in Jack's eyes. 'Sounds riveting. You don't share your fiancé's passion…for stamps?'

She scowled. How he loved to harp on that word *passion*! 'A couple can have individual interests,' she growled. 'A lot of people find stamp collecting *extremely* riveting.' Even her best friend Melanie was a keen stamp collector, though she was nowhere near as involved as Brendan.

'Quite so. Each to his own. So…he's passionate about stamps *and* Gilbert and Sullivan…' He paused. 'Sounds a passionate man…' A silvery gleam lit his eye. '*Is* he?'

She inhaled a lungful of air. 'Did you want to take a look at my injuries or not?' she snapped. 'I have things to do.'

'Me too. Let's step into this room…' Jack indicated

her makeshift studio. The door was wide open. 'We'll have a better light.'

She shrugged. 'If you like.'

As he followed her in, Jack caught sight of her easel, over by the window. She'd angled Melanie's portrait to catch the light, so they could only see the back of it from where they were.

'Let's move closer to the window. I'll avert my eyes,' Jack promised, 'if that's another of your nude males. Your fiancé, no doubt?'

'It's my flatmate, Melanie,' she bit out. 'I've just finished it. There's no need to look the other way,' she added with a tinge of sarcasm. 'Feel free to give an opinion.' As an avid art collector and a friend of Selwyn Dodd, he must know something about art.

'Thanks...I will. But first things first.'

He drew her over to the light, his hand brushing her arm, raising the fine hairs on her skin. Swinging her round, he took her face in both hands and gently tilted her chin upward. He peered into her eyes. Deep, deep into her eyes.

Tension gripped her. She couldn't breathe. She couldn't even blink. She badly wanted to swallow, but was afraid to move a muscle. *He's just a doctor, doing his job,* she thought wildly, her heart fluttering like a trapped bird. Then, more frantically, *Think of Charlotte...think of Brendan...think of your wedding day.*

But she *couldn't* think! Not with Jack so close.

In a brutal attempt at clinical detachment, she focused her mind on the eyes gazing into hers, taking steely note of every tiny fleck of light and colour in the vivid blue.

It didn't work. All it did was to swamp her with the

heady sensation that she was drowning...lique-fying...losing control...

She tore his hands from her face and stepped back...almost upsetting her easel.

'That's enough!' Her voice shook. 'I'm perfectly all right!'

He held up his hands to show that she had nothing to fear from him. 'Can't you bear me to touch you, Kate...even professionally?' He gave a soft laugh. 'Or is the problem that you *like* me touching you...more than you hate it?'

She snatched in an outraged breath, so incensed that words failed her. She glanced up at him shakily. Warily. There was a disturbing glitter in his eye. Of satisfaction? Triumph? It unnerved her. *He* unnerved her. She had the feeling he could see into her very soul, into the hidden recesses of her heart. Into places she didn't want to look herself...*refused* to look herself.

He gave another wicked chuckle. 'But I mustn't tease,' he said easily. 'You're an engaged woman, about to be married. A woman in love with her...absent fiancé. May I take a look at your work now?' he asked coolly, turning to her easel.

'Make it quick,' she cracked out, thankful for the respite. Her nerves felt shredded, her body overheated, quivering with nervous tension. 'I have wedding arrangements to see to,' she reminded him, grinding the words out.

'How could I forget?' The teasing note had gone. His voice was flat now, resigned.

She should have felt relieved, but instead she felt unbearably weighed down...empty. But for her sister, things might have been different. Jack's 'golden mermaid' might have waited for him. Jack might have *asked* her to wait.

Well, it was too late now. She was committed to Brendan. Happy with Brendan. And there were no ghosts to sour her relationship with *him*...or to upset her parents.

Jack examined the portrait for a long moment in silence. An achingly tense silence, filled with floating images from the past.

She realised she was holding her breath. Didn't he like it?

'Attractive girl,' he said finally, and she felt an odd little jab pierce her. Now that she'd convinced him that she was marrying another man, was he already looking elsewhere?

She frowned. He wasn't Melanie's type at all! Dear Mel wouldn't be able to cope for five seconds with a dynamo like Jack Savage!

'Yes, she's a lovely girl,' she agreed, secretly relieved that her close friend was away for the weekend. Jack would eat poor Mel alive! And then he'd lose interest, no doubt, and go waltzing off after a more meaty challenge, leaving dear Mel with a broken heart. The way he'd left Charlotte—a far tougher prospect—with a broken heart.

She jumped, her breath whooshing out in relief, as the phone in the hall started ringing again.

'Well...looks as if he *must* be passionate about you,' Jack drawled. 'Two phone calls in ten minutes.'

Kate hoped fervently that it *was* Brendan, ringing back to say he'd changed his mind about staying away the extra night. Could he have sensed her emotional turmoil? Her need for him? Had he decided to give up his dinner on Sunday night after all, and come rushing home to her instead?

She sprinted to the phone, hoping that for once Brendan *had* used extra-sensory powers! 'Hullo?'

The hope in her eyes faded when she heard her father's brusque voice. 'Ah, Kate, glad I caught you.'

'Hullo, Dad.' She tried to inject brightness into her voice. 'How was the conference?'

'Fruitful.' He brushed that aside. 'Kate, your mother's not feeling the best, and I—'

'What's wrong?' Kate cut in. Her mother was never ill. The colds, viruses and sore throats that beleaguered everyone else always seemed to pass her by. Or she managed to brush them aside without making a fuss.

'She has a bad headache. I've dosed her up and she's resting in a darkened room. But this afternoon's off as far as working on the seating plan for the wedding goes. Best to leave it anyway, until Brendan's back.'

Her father, after initially being less than enthusiastic about her choice of future partner, had come to like and approve of Brendan. He saw him as steady and reliable and financially stable. An achiever, in his quiet way. He would have preferred her to marry someone with a medical or even a legal background—someone who had more in common, intellectually and philosophically, with the Warren-Smiths and their peers—but he knew that Brendan would never disgrace or embarrass the family. Or hurt his daughter.

She swallowed, imagining what might have happened if she'd still been free...and had actually encouraged Jack Savage's advances. Top neurosurgeon or not, her father would never have accepted her involvement with Jonathan Savage, let alone welcomed him into the family. And she couldn't have hurt him that way, causing him more pain and anguish. And bitter anger too, no doubt.

Regardless of all that, Jack was a doctor—a specialist surgeon—and she'd vowed never to get involved with a man like her father.

'Never mind about the wedding plans.' She brushed her father's comment aside. 'Dad, I'll still come over—'

'No! Kate, there's nothing you can do. She just needs rest and quiet.' Her father never called her 'love' or 'darling'—endearments didn't come easily to him—but at least, since he'd been reunited with his wife and younger daughter, he'd been calling her Kate instead of Catherine. 'I'll be here at home all day,' he assured her, 'if your mother needs anything. Or gets any worse.'

'Well, if there's anything I can do, or if Mum needs me, don't hesitate to let me know at once. Ring me on my mobile,' Kate told him. 'I have to go the hospital to pick up my car, and to the jeweller's to pick up my ring. I was coming over to your place after that, but now…well, you know how to reach me.'

'Yes. Thanks, Kate.' Her father hung up. He never chatted for the sake of chatting. Normally he was too busy, or his mind too preoccupied with work, but today, Kate thought worriedly, he seemed more preoccupied with her mother than with work. Maybe he was more concerned about her than he'd let on.

Poor Mum, she thought, her heart going out to the mother who'd always been there for her. As far as she knew, her mother had never suffered from headaches before. If she had, she'd never mentioned them.

She felt for her father too. Since the loss of his beloved elder daughter, there *had* been a noticeable change in him. Though still reticent, he was no longer the same coldly remote, distant father he'd been in the past. He'd grown closer to his wife and remaining daughter, and had shown them, by a softer attitude generally, if not in words, that he did care for them. The very fact that he was staying at home to care for her mother, when in the past he would have been too busy and left it to Kate, attested to his new-found humanity.

'Something's wrong with your mother?'

Kate jumped. She'd forgotten that Jack was still there!

'Mum has a bad headache, that's all.' She sighed. She hoped it *was* all.

'I'm sorry to hear that, Kate,' Jack said, and she flinched at the caring note in his voice. It brought back memories she didn't want brought back. 'You were planning to go over to your parents' place, I gather...and now you can't. Poor Kate,' he sympathised, without any discernible mockery. 'Your flatmate's away. Your fiancé's away. And now you won't even have your parents for company.'

Her nerve-ends sprang to full alert.

'I don't think you should be alone, Kate.'

Her head jerked back. 'I *like* being on my own. I *like* having time to myself,' she said, rather too forcibly. 'It gives me a chance to do all sorts of things I don't normally have time for.' She was ready to reel off a list, but he didn't give her the chance.

'Have you had lunch?'

Her stomach lurched. She frowned. Wasn't he listening to her? 'I'm not hungry. I had a late breakfast.'

'Right. Then you'll be ready for an early dinner.'

She eyed him warily, hoping that purposeful look in

his eye didn't mean he wanted her to have dinner with *him*.

'I have things to do this afternoon...'

'Yes, I heard. So have I. I'll drive you to the hospital to pick up your car. I have to see a couple of patients.' As her eyes flicked over his tennis gear, he said dismissively, 'I've a change of clothes at the hospital. While I'm doing my rounds, Kate, you can go and pick up your engagement ring and do whatever else you need to do. I'll pick you up back here at six and we'll find somewhere casual to have a relaxing drink and an early meal.'

It was Dr Savage at his most masterful. Expecting her to meekly give in. Why was she even hesitating? She'd be mad to accept! Dinner with Jack Savage? And what about *afterwards*? Her heartbeat went haywire.

'Look...I'll drop you home at an early hour and I won't come in,' Jack promised, as if uncannily reading her mind. Jack was good at reading minds, she thought with a frown. 'You need company...someone to keep a caring eye on you...and who better than a fellow doctor?'

Lethal company. A lethal carer.

'Why waste your time on another man's bride-to-be?' she challenged hoarsely, wanting to remind him that she was committed to another man.

'I don't consider keeping an eye on a friend a waste of time,' Jack returned coolly. 'You said you wanted us to be friends, Kate...well, here's your chance to show you meant it. Just friends,' he stressed, a taunting light in his eye.

She gulped. He was throwing her words back at her...the words she'd seized on last night to cover up her reaction to his kiss. If she refused his offer of friendship, he'd suspect that she really *had* felt more than she'd admitted to. And she hadn't! She didn't! It was just the memory of her feelings for him five years ago that had affected her for a few crazy seconds, until reality returned. That nasty blow to the head hadn't helped.

'I can't go out to dinner looking as if my fiancé has bashed me,' she argued, remembering her bruises.

He dismissed the excuse with a short laugh. 'Doctors are always getting attacked by patients. Brush your curls forward if it bothers you, or dab something on it. Now...remove that artist's smock and grab your purse and keys. We're going. My patients are waiting for me.'

He was reminding her that he was a doctor, first and foremost. *Her* doctor too, for today. A friend, a carer, nothing more.

Well, she might as well accept a lift to the hospital to pick up her car. On the way there she could think of an excuse to get out of dinner tonight.

By the time Jack swung his BMW into the hospital car park, she had her excuse ready. She couldn't think why she hadn't thought of it earlier.

Because the idea of a casual evening meal with Jack had almost seduced her? Not Jack himself...heavens no! She firmly rejected any question of seduction—on either side. Last night, when he'd kissed her, Jack hadn't known about Brendan or her imminent wedding day. Now he did, and his invitation for this evening was simply to show her they could still be friends.

Could they? Despite the simmering chemistry between them? Despite the recurring spectre of Charlotte? A shivery ripple ran down her spine. Safer to keep right away from him.

'Thanks for dropping me off, Jack,' she said as he nosed his car into his reserved parking bay and pulled up. 'Better forget about dinner,' she added lightly. 'I want to call in home and cook a meal for my parents. My mother won't feel up to it. And my father's hopeless in that area.'

His hand stopped her before she could open the car door. 'I understood that your father had a woman in daily to do his cooking and cleaning.'

Her stomach jumped. How could he possibly know that? Charlotte? 'That—that was when he was separated from my mother,' she floundered. 'She—Anna—doesn't come every day now. She—she only comes during the week.' *Or any time her parents needed her.*

'Kate, get on your mobile and ring your father now,' Jack said calmly. 'Make the offer, by all means. If he accepts, well and good. Knowing you'll have company for the evening is all I ever wanted for you, Kate.'

She flushed, hearing no mocking undercurrent. This was the thoughtful, caring Jack she'd known five years ago. He had no wicked intentions. No hidden agenda. He was just concerned about her. *She* was the one with the problem. The hang-ups. The lurid imaginings.

Why? she wondered in despair. In a couple of weeks she'd be walking down the aisle with Brendan. In a few minutes she'd be picking up Brendan's engagement ring…and Jack knew that, and would expect to see her wearing it the next time they met. It didn't bother him. He just wanted to be friends. He only wanted to keep an eye on her because she'd suffered a punch to the head and he knew she had no one else to turn to for the time being.

Why was she making such a big thing of it?

'Well...I'll just check.' She gave in reluctantly and pulled out her mobile phone, resigned to receiving a polite knockback from her father and having to spend the evening with Jack.

Her father answered at the first ring. 'Yes?' Short and terse.

'Dad, it's just me. How's Mum?'

'Ah, Kate, I was about to ring *you*. She's not good. Her headache's worse. Much worse. I'm taking her to hospital.'

Hospital? Alarm raced through her. 'To Eastern General?' she asked quickly. 'Dad, I'll meet you there—'

'No...not there. I'm taking her to St Mark's. I've just spoken to Magnus Barratt and he's coming in specially to take a look at her. He's going to run some tests.'

Her heart chilled. *Tests?* Overseen by Magnus Barratt himself? That sounded ominous. But there was another problem. 'You're bringing her *here*...to St Mark's?' *Jack* worked at St Mark's! Worse, he was assistant neurosurgeon to Magnus Barratt! Her father wouldn't be aware of that yet. He'd been in Hong Kong for the past week. The two might meet...

'St Mark's has the top neurosurgeon in Australia,' her father rapped back. 'And I know Magnus personally. It's just a precaution at this stage, Kate. I want to be sure it's nothing serious. It could be a lot of things, and I want your mother to be diagnosed by the best man. You're there *now*, did you say? At St Mark's? I thought you had the weekend off.'

'I just came to pick up my car. I'll wait here for you—'

'Look, let's not panic, Kate, or panic your mother. It'll

take a while to run the tests, and Magnus and I will be with her. You go and do whatever you have to do. I promise I'll call you when I know something.' With that he hung up.

Kate's shoulders slumped. Her father must be really worried if he'd decided to bring her mother here to St Mark's rather than his own hospital…and if he'd summoned Magnus Barratt on a weekend.

'Your mother's worse?'

Her head jerked round, her eyes meeting Jack's, noting the concern in the deep blue. She nodded mutely.

'And your father's bringing her here…to St Mark's?' Jack frowned, seeming more worried about her mother, it struck Kate, than wary of a confrontation with her father…though he had plenty of reason, she thought with a sigh, to be wary of meeting Chester Warren-Smith. She wondered how her father would react if they did come face to face. Hopefully, he'd be too anxious about her mother to create a scene at the hospital.

Should she have warned her father, Kate wondered, so he'd be prepared? But he hadn't given her a chance…

'Yes.' Tears gathered behind her eyes at the thought of her mother. 'Her headache's so bad that Dad's asked Magnus Barratt to take a look at her and run some tests. Dr Barratt's coming in specially.' A tremor ran through her. She was already imagining the worst possible scenarios, as doctors tended to do.

'Well, she'll be in the best hands.' Jack assured her. 'Let's hope it's nothing serious.'

She nodded, clenching her hands together in an attempt to stop their trembling. She jumped as she felt Jack's hands close over hers. For a moment she let their warmth and comfort seep into her, then she slid her hands free.

'Thanks for dropping me off, Jack. And...and for offering to look after me.' For the first time her eyes showed regret at missing out on having dinner with Jack. The idea didn't sound so daunting any more—it even sounded positively inviting—now that she had more serious problems to worry about.

As she opened the car door and stepped out, she heard Jack's voice from behind. 'That's what friends are for.' He jumped out too...a powerfully athletic figure in his tennis shorts and shirt. 'You're coming into the hospital now, Kate, to wait for your parents?'

She shook her head. 'Dad wants to be with Dr Barratt while the tests are being done...and they'll take a while.' She sighed. The boys' club again. Second-year residents—daughters—would only be in the way. And her presence might alarm her mother.

'I'll come back in an hour or so,' she decided aloud. Whether her father wanted her there or not. She *needed* to be there...needed to be close to both her parents when the test results became known.

She would pick up her engagement ring, pop into the shoe shop nearby to buy a pair of shoes for her wedding day—something she'd been putting off—and then she'd come back. In the meantime, she'd leave her mobile phone on, just in case her father needed to contact her.

She shivered.

'Jack...' She delayed a moment longer before heading for her car. 'If you run into my father...' She hesitated. 'I—I haven't had a chance yet to tell him you're working here,' she reminded him. 'I...it might come as a bit of a shock.'

He would have had more of a shock, it occurred to her, if he'd seen his daughter walk into the hospital with Jack Savage!

'I hardly think we're likely to come to blows at a time like this.' Jack gave a shrug, seeming unconcerned. 'We're both professional doctors, Kate.' A wry smile touched his lips. 'Doctors don't let their personal feelings intrude when they meet professionally. We've been trained to conceal our emotions, remember?'

His eyes caught hers for a second, and she swallowed at the glint of irony in the keen blue depths.

'The heartless, remote specialist,' she murmured with a tinge of bitterness. Both her father and Jack had been guilty of the label. Jack with her sister, her father with her mother and herself.

Jack's brow lowered, a flatness replacing the silvery gleam in his eye. 'Just because we conceal our emotions, Kate, doesn't mean we don't have them.'

The heaviness in his tone made her glance sharply up him. Was he talking about her sister? Had he felt something for Charlotte after all? Did he finally regret having turned his back on her?

'Sometimes we show our feelings too late,' she muttered, and swung away from him, a heavy weight settling in her stomach.

CHAPTER NINE

JUST over an hour later, Kate was back at the hospital. She caught a lift and pushed the button for the seventh floor, where Neurosurgery was. On the way up the lift stopped at the fifth floor, Pathology.

The door opened and Jack Savage stepped in.

'Jack! You're still here!' She almost pounced on him. 'Have you seen Dr Barratt? Have you heard anything?'

'About your mother?' Jack turned to press a button to send the lift on its way. 'I believe she's still having tests. Dr Barratt may be able to tell you more.'

He sounded a bit guarded, she thought, her heartbeat faltering. He'd obviously been up to Neurosurgery and seen Dr Barratt. Or met him in Nuclear Medicine earlier. Of course, Jack wouldn't tell her anything, even if he knew. Her mother was Magnus Barratt's patient.

But surely, if all appeared to be well so far, he could have given her some reassurances.

Perhaps it was too soon. She sighed.

'Have you seen my father?' She couldn't hold the breathless question back.

Jack's mouth curled in a rueful smile. But there was no smile in his eyes. 'We met…yes. Don't worry, Kate,' he drawled, 'your father didn't go for my throat…though it looked for a moment as if he might. Would you have cared if he had?' His eyes mocked her.

She skipped the loaded question. 'What did he say?' she pressed. 'Did he…say anything about Charlotte?' she ventured. 'Or ask if—if you'd met me?' She wasn't sure why it was so important to know. 'What did *you* say…to him?'

Jack shrugged, and said dryly, 'I merely acknowledged him with a polite, 'Dr Warren-Smith.' And your father, rather less politely, said, ''I thought you intended to do heart surgery?'''

'Did you tell him *why* you'd switched to neurosurgery?' Kate breathed, hoping that Jack hadn't inflamed the situation by telling her father what he'd intimated to *her* all those years ago—that he'd wanted to avoid the possibility of working with her father.

Jack's mouth twisted again, this time not so pleasantly. 'I told your father that heart surgery was too crowded.'

Her heart sank. To her father, that would have been like waving a red flag to a bull! Why couldn't Jack simply have said that neurosurgery held more appeal…or posed more of a challenge? Or, better still, told her father that he'd been considering the feelings of the Warren-Smith family by choosing a different field?

Her chest rose and fell. She'd been half hoping that Jack might even have apologised to her father for hurting Charlotte—for unknowingly hurting her—and tried to make peace with him.

But not Jack. There would be no bending from Jack. No olive branch. He was still as uncaring, as unfeeling as she'd always thought him. At least where her sister was concerned.

'My father must have loved hearing that,' she said caustically as the lift came to a stop at the seventh floor. If Jack had only bent a little, her father might—just might—have softened too. But Jack continued to act as if he'd done nothing wrong. He simply didn't care!

'What did he say?' she asked heavily as the door slid open.

'Nothing. Magnus intervened, declaring that he was delighted I'd chosen *his* field, and that he was hoping I'd take over from him when he retired. And then he changed the subject. To more immediate concerns.'

Her mother?

'Keep your chin up, Kate,' Jack tossed back at her as he headed off towards his suite, leaving her to seek out Magnus Barratt's secretary.

Keep your chin up... She gulped, a lump filling her throat. Was that a hint that she would shortly be needing all her strength?

It was bad news. Shocking news. Her mother had a brain tumour. It was exerting dangerous pressure and required an immediate operation. Magnus Barratt didn't need to add *a life-saving operation*.

The next few hours passed in a nightmarish haze. Kate stayed close to her father, who was outwardly stoic but plainly terrified underneath. She could see it in his eyes, hear it in his voice, feel it in the tremor of his hands.

And he had reason to be terrified, she thought with a shiver. Dr Barratt had spelt out the dangers. Although the tumour appeared to be benign, it would be a delicate operation, with some very real dangers. He'd spelt them out so they'd be prepared. There was the possibility of blindness, paralysis, fits, a stroke. He hadn't needed to add the other possibility, a danger in any delicate operation. *Death.*

Kate's mother was the bravest of all of them. Before being wheeled into the operating room, she gripped her husband's hand and whispered, 'You're not to worry, dearest…Magnus will take care of me. Just remember…I love you. I've always loved you. I always will.'

She had some words for Kate too. 'And you, Kate…I love you so much. We're so lucky to have you…'

'Not as lucky as we are to have you,' Kate said huskily, trying not to show the fear that was twisting inside her.

As she bent down to kiss her mother's bravely smiling lips, her mother whispered urgently, 'You'll take care of your father, won't you, Kate?'

'Of course I will.' Kate knew what her mother meant. Not just during the operation, but afterwards…should anything go wrong. Always thinking of others, never herself, she thought, fighting back tears.

But her mother had more to say. 'Whatever happens, go ahead with the wedding, darling…if it's what you really want. Be happy, Kate.'

The rather strange words *'if it's what you really want'* didn't really sink in until later. Just then, nothing else mattered to Kate but her mother.

'I love you, too, Mum. You just get well.'

As the trolley vanished into OR 5, an anguished whisper was dragged from her father's throat. 'I can't lose her too. I couldn't bear it.'

Kate's breath stopped. It was the first time in her whole life that her father had stripped his heart bare to *her*, his younger daughter. After Charlotte's death he'd been visibly affected—devastated—but he'd never spoken of the pain he was suffering, never voiced his feelings aloud, other than to vent his anger at the absent Jonathan Savage.

Too choked up to say a word, she slipped an arm through her father's, and squeezed gently. She drew him over to a padded seat, where they sank down side by side. He'd insisted, beforehand, on staying close to the operating room, even though he knew the delicate operation was going to take hours.

Mum's in the best hands, Kate kept telling herself. Magnus Barratt is the top neurosurgeon in the country, and he has a great team.

She knew that the hospital's top anaesthetist was on hand, even though it was a weekend and he'd been summoned at short notice. She knew that each nurse and technician present was highly qualified and competent. And today, instead of his chief resident assisting, Dr Barratt had announced that Jack Savage, his talented protégé, would be working alongside him.

Her father hadn't liked *that*, but he'd voiced no objection, knowing that the operation was urgent and that Jack, being a qualified neurosurgeon, should, by rights, be more skilled than any resident. Heaven help Jack, Kate thought, if a mistake was made and it was put down to *him*! But she mustn't even *think* about mistakes. The operation was dangerous and delicate enough.

As the first hour dragged by, and darkness began to fall outside, she had food brought up from the canteen for them both. They each made an effort, but only to encourage the other. Neither of them was hungry. Kate made sure she kept the coffee coming, using the doctors' coffee room nearby.

During the second long hour they were startled by a familiar alarm, followed by a message on the PA: 'Code Blue, Code Blue, OR 5... Code Blue, Code Blue, OR 5.'

Kate sat upright, her blood chilling. OR 5 was the operating room where her mother was! And Code Blue was the code for cardiac arrest!

'My God, your mother's gone into arrest!' Her father sprang to his feet. 'I have to go to her!'

'Dad, no! You can't go into the OR!' Kate grabbed his arm as doctors and nurses came running in answer to the call. 'They know what to do.' There was always a cardiac arrest team on stand-by at the hospital, even at weekends.

'It's my *wife*, for heaven's sake!' Her father tore his arm free. 'And I'm a heart specialist…I'm going in!'

'Well, I'm coming with you!'

They both made a dive for OR 5.

In the ante-room, a nurse stopped them. 'You can't come in here—'

'Do you know who I am?' roared Chester Warren-Smith. 'It's my wife in there! If she's in arrest—'

'It's not your wife!' the nurse cut in. 'It's Dr Barratt. He was operating and he—he suddenly clutched his chest and staggered back. A couple of us helped him into the recovery room next door, just as he collapsed. The cardiac team are working on him now…everything's under control.'

'*And what about my wife?*' Chester bellowed, more concerned about her now than the chief neurosurgeon's heart attack. 'She's supposed to be having delicate *brain* surgery! Can it safely be put off until—?'

'It can't wait, Doctor. There's no need to worry,' the nurse assured him. 'Dr Savage has taken over.'

'*What?* I don't want him doing the—'

'Dr Savage is a highly skilled neurosurgeon, Doctor. With the operation already underway, there was no choice. Please, Doctor, you must wait outside. Your wife couldn't be in better hands.' She appealed to Kate. 'Perhaps a cup of tea would help, Kate, while you're both waiting…'

'I don't *want* a cup of tea.' Chester scowled at the hapless nurse, but he let Kate steer him back outside, where he slumped down with his head in his hands.

'What hope does she have now?' It was a bitter groan. 'Damn Magnus Barratt! How could he have a heart attack *now*? Doesn't he have check-ups? He's left my wife in the hands of a cold-blooded charlatan!'

'Ja— Dr Savage's no charlatan, Dad.' Kate heard herself defending Jack. 'He's a brilliant neurosurgeon—everyone says so. He's worked with the top neurosurgeons in America…with the very top man in New York.' She was surprised at how heatedly she was standing up for him.

'And he's a much younger and fitter man than Dr Barratt,' she consoled her father. 'His hand will be steadier, his eyes sharper. Dad, he really cares about his patients. Ask anybody. I know he hasn't been back in Australia for long, but he's already highly regarded here at the hospital.'

It was true…he was. And not just for his stunning good looks! She'd heard about Jack's remarkable successes this past week, and his outstanding achievements overseas had been written up in medical journals and talked about since his arrival.

She just hoped, for all their sakes, that Jack would live up to his glittering reputation.

But—she swallowed, nibbling nervously on her lip—this was an operation that even the top man in the field had deemed highly delicate and potentially dangerous. Even if her mother came through the operation, would she come through it unscathed? If she didn't, her father would blame Jack Savage; Kate knew it, whether it was his direct fault or not.

A male nurse came out of OR 5 shortly afterwards

and rushed off to Pathology. Kate avoided her father's eye, guessing that the nurse was rushing to have a sample tested to find out if the tumour was benign or malignant. She shuddered. What if it was malignant? What if Jack wasn't able to remove all of it? What if he damaged—?

She shut her eyes, cutting off the frightening thoughts.

It was another three hours before they heard any more...other than the good news that Magnus Barratt was apparently recovering well in the Coronary Care Unit. Keen to give her over-wrought father something else to think about, Kate tried to persuade him to go and see Dr Barratt while they were waiting. Even though Magnus must have learned by now that his untimely heart attack hadn't disrupted the operation, it would reassure him, she told her father, to hear it from him.

'It won't take a minute, Dad,' she urged. 'They probably won't let you stay more than a minute anyway,' she added, secretly hoping that Magnus, if he was awake and able to speak, would do some reassuring in return—about Jack Savage. Her father badly needed it. He was a nervous wreck, and hardly bothering to hide it.

'But the operation could be over any time now—' he began to argue.

'You'll be back in a few minutes. Off you go... Magnus must be feeling terrible about what happened. If there's any news I'll call you immediately, I promise.'

He finally—reluctantly—agreed. As she watched his bowed figure lumber off, she felt for him as never before. He'd always been so straight, so strong, so sure of himself, almost invincible. Now he looked like an old man, forlorn and helpless, with the weight of the world on his shoulders.

Once he'd vanished from sight, she let her own shoul-

ders droop. Buoying up her father had kept her own
spirits at a reasonably high level, but now that she had
no one depending on her strength, she found her morale
crumbling, her fears tumbling back.

How much longer was it going to be before they knew
anything? It had been five long hours already. Had
something gone wrong? Was Jack having trouble with
some delicate aspect of the operation? Or was the operation already over, and her mother was failing to wake
up—which must be any neurosurgeon's worst nightmare? What if she was in a coma? What if she was
blind? What if—?

'Ah, there you are, Kate.'

Her breath choked in her throat. Jack Savage was
coming towards her in his pale blue scrub gown, his
surgical mask round his neck. He was *smiling*.

'Your mother's fine,' he said, before she could ask.
'The operation was a total success. She's awake and
there are no signs of any neurological problems. She can
see, hear and feel...and has movement in her arms and
legs.'

'Oh, Jack! Jack, you *genius*!' She was so relieved, so
ecstatic, so overcome with gratitude and amazement at
what Jack had done for her mother that she hurled herself at him, throwing her arms round his neck.

'Thank you, thank you, thank you!' she gasped. 'I
knew you'd do it, Jack. I knew it would be all right! Oh,
Jack, it's wonderful news. I'm so relieved!'

Relieved for her mother, relieved for her father, relieved for herself, and almost as relieved for Jack. He'd
taken over from the top man in the country and produced
a miracle!

Before she realised what she was doing she'd grabbed

his head in both hands and was planting kisses all over his face—his cheeks, his eyes, his jaw, his mouth...

She became dimly aware that his own arms had folded around her and that the pliant lips under hers were responding...coming alive...moving against hers. For a crazy moment she let herself revel in the feel and the warmth of them, unable to draw back—until the sound of footsteps approaching from behind brought her head back sharply.

As she jerked a look round, letting her hands slide from Jack's shadowed jaw, she met her father's eyes.

He looked stunned, as if he couldn't believe what he was witnessing. But there was a burning hope and anxiety in his eyes too, that overrode the shock, or the disapproval, or whatever it was. His apprehension turned to joyful relief as her lips burst into a smile.

'Dad, Mum's all right!' she cried, whirling round to hug him. She repeated what Jack had just told her.

Her father's heartfelt relief was palpable, elation lighting his usually austere face. As if not daring to believe it, he turned to Jack for confirmation.

'It's true, Dr Warren-Smith. Everything went well. The tumour was benign, and we've removed all of it. Your wife should make a full recovery.'

'Thank you.' Chester seemed to hesitate for just a second, then he did something Kate had never expected to see. He held out his hand to Jack Savage. 'May I see her?' he asked as he pumped the hand of the man he'd hated for so long.

Jack nodded. 'They'll be wheeling her out in just a minute, to take her down to ICU,' he said. 'She'll be asleep—she drifted back to sleep straight away—so you won't be able to talk to her...but don't worry, it's a

normal, healthy sleep, and should last until she wakes
up fresh tomorrow morning.'

Kate noted that he hadn't said, *hopefully she'll wake
up fresh*. As a doctor, she was as aware as Jack and her
father must be that the risks weren't entirely over. She
wondered if Jack felt as confident as he sounded.

'When you've seen her, you can both go home and
have a good night's sleep yourselves,' Jack advised.
'Ah...here she comes now.'

Kate felt a thickness welling in her throat as her
mother was wheeled out, her head swathed in bandages,
her eyes closed, her face pale and peaceful. She let her
father rush forward first. As Chester bent over his wife,
she heard Jack's voice at her ear.

'Are you going home with your father, Kate? Or back
to your place?'

As she flicked a startled look round—*why would he
want to know that?*—he added sardonically, 'I'm surprised your fiancé isn't here with you by now, holding
your hand. Is he on his way back or not?'

Her hand fluttered to her throat. *Brendan!* She felt her
face flood with a guilty heat. She hadn't given her fiancé
a thought over the past traumatic hours. Not consciously,
at least. Somewhere in the back of her mind she must
have been thinking of him...been dimly aware of him
in another city, immersed in his beloved stamps...too
far away to be of any help, any comfort.

She frowned, knowing that Jack must have seen her
guilty reaction, and must be thinking, *Out of sight, out
of mind*.

She jerked a shoulder. That wasn't how it was at all!
She'd just been so worried about her mother...so concerned about her father.

'Brendan's a judge, for the first time, at a very important stamp fair,' she informed him in her crispest tone. 'Besides, there was nothing he could do here, even if he could have made it back in time. Everything happened so quickly.' She hissed in an exasperated breath, realising she was babbling, making needless excuses. 'My father needed my support,' she said tightly.

'And who's supporting *you*?' Jack moved a step closer, dropping his voice even lower. 'If you were my girl, I'd want to be here for you. I'd make sure I was. I'd put you ahead of everything else in my life. And I'd want *you* to share everything with *me*—your lows as well as your highs—because anything affecting you would affect me equally as much.'

A violent tremor shook through her. She couldn't meet his eye, not wanting to see the mockery there, or worse, the concern…the warmth…the caring he'd shown for her before. She knew that how Jack Savage looked or felt shouldn't bother her, but it did…and the fact that it did bothered her even more.

Without a word, she swung away, joining her father at her mother's side, leaning over the trolley to brush a kiss over her mother's pale cheek.

'Love you, Mum,' she whispered, and kept her eye on her mother's tranquil face as the trolley was finally whisked away.

'Come on, Dad.' She caught his arm. 'I'm taking you home.'

Jack, she noticed out of the corner of her eye, had disappeared.

She let her breath out in a whispery sigh, feeling surprised—disturbed—at the peculiar yearning she felt.

CHAPTER TEN

WHEN she came back to St Mark's the next morning, with her father, Jack was already there, meeting them at the door of the ICU as the sister-in-charge led them in.

Kate's eyes swept anxiously over Jack's face, trying to read his expression before her father asked, 'How is she?' The sister had only told them that her mother was awake and that Dr Savage would fill them in on her progress.

Kate thought Jack looked a bit tired, his eyes smudged as if he hadn't had much sleep after his long operation the night before. She found herself wondering what could have disturbed his badly needed sleep. Had he been worrying about her mother? About the state of his fragile truce with her father? About *her*?

Her eyes shadowed a little. Just because she'd stayed awake herself for hours, mulling over what he'd said to her yesterday, and shamefully reliving that impulsive kiss of hers last night, it didn't mean *he'd* been thinking about them too.

His ready smile wiped her idle musings from her mind. Surely he wouldn't be smiling like that if her mother had developed any problems since last night?

'Your wife's continuing to do well, Doctor,' Jack assured her father. 'She was sitting up having breakfast a short time ago. We couldn't be happier with her progress so far.'

So far... He was still being cautious, Kate noted, sliding her tongue along lips which had gone dry at the sight of him.

'That's good news.' Her father's voice was gruffly polite. He still wasn't comfortable feeling indebted to Jack Savage, Kate reflected with a sigh.

'Sister Marsh will take you to her,' Jack said, standing aside.

'You go first, Dad,' Kate whispered, expecting Jack to turn on his heel and stride off. 'I'll give you a few minutes alone with Mum before I see her.'

Her father gave her arm a grateful squeeze and moved off with the nurse. Kate felt a strange shivery sensation as she realised that Jack was still there, his eyes searching her face—rather too intently for comfort.

'Have you slept at all, Kate?'

Suddenly finding it difficult to breathe, she flicked a cautious glance up at him. How could he tell that she'd barely slept? Even her own father hadn't noticed. But then, her father seldom noticed such things. He seldom noticed much at all outside his specialised field of cardiac surgery. She'd learned to make allowances for him, putting his lack of awareness down to the demands of being a busy, dedicated surgeon—Sydney's top cardiac surgeon.

Yet here was Jack Savage, just as busy, just as dedicated, noticing and caring about people who weren't even his patients. Noticing things about *her* that even her future husband would be unlikely to notice!

She wrenched her gaze from the concern in Jack's, dismayed at the way her thoughts were going, and appalled at the erratic behaviour of her heart. She couldn't very well admit that she hadn't slept because she'd been thinking about *him*! He was the last man she ought to be thinking about, two weeks before her wedding day.

She groaned—and realised as the sound rumbled from her throat that she'd groaned aloud.

'Kate, what's wrong?' Jack caught her arm, and she leapt back as if stung. His touch was the last thing she wanted at this moment! 'You're not still worried about your mother, are you? I assure you—'

'I was thinking about my *wedding* day!' she burst out, suddenly desperate to remind him of it. Or desperate to remind herself!

'Oh?' His voice chilled, and a pang quivered through her as she heard it. 'You're still going ahead with it, then? Even though your mother won't be well enough to be there? She'll be in hospital for close on two weeks, you realise, and will need to rest and be careful for some time after that.'

Kate dragged stricken eyes back to his face. 'I—I don't know what to do!' she admitted, almost in a wail. 'Mum wants me to go ahead with the wedding, whether she can be there or not. If I cancel—postpone it,' she was quick to amend, 'she'll be upset. She'll blame herself. It might cause her to—to—' She gulped off the rest, unable to put her fear into words.

It was then that she remembered something. Something her mother had said to her, just before her operation. She'd urged Kate to go ahead with the wedding... *'if it's what you really want.'* Why on earth, Kate wondered, would her mother say a thing like that to her, so close to her wedding day? Did she have doubts too? *Too?*

Her hand slid up to her throat, where a pulse was beating madly. Where in the world had *that* thought come from? *She* had no doubts...she didn't! If Brendan had been here, the thought would never have surfaced. She was just feeling sorry for herself. And she could blame Jack Savage for that. All his talk about supporting her and being there for her if she were his girl…

'Your mother's a brave, fine woman, Kate, and a lovely person.' Jack spoke as if he'd known her mother for weeks rather than only since yesterday, when she'd come in for tests. Her sister, of course, must have talked to Jack about her mother. Charlotte had loved her mother, perhaps as much as Kate did, even though she'd sided with her father during their parents' separation.

Or had Jack simply summed up her mother's character in the brief time he'd known her? Her mother was a warm, lovable, giving person, whose caring and concern for others shone out of her, endearing her to everyone she met.

'From what I've come to know of your mother,' Jack added softly, 'I can understand her not wanting to disrupt your wedding plans, Kate. But I'm sure that, deep down, she'd want to be at her daughter's wedding…especially now that she's come through the operation and is likely to make a full recovery.'

Kate slid a look up at him through her lashes. He was right. Reluctant as she was to agree with him on the subject of her wedding day, after the sly digs he'd made about her relationship with Brendan, he *was* right. If she postponed the wedding for a few months, her mother would be fully recovered by then and could be there, as the mother of the bride should be. And it would give *her* more time too…to prepare for it.

She didn't want to dwell on the reason *why* she needed more time to prepare for her wedding. She only knew that it would take some of this awful pressure off her and give her some breathing space.

She straightened her shoulders. 'I'll talk it over with

Brendan. He'll be home tomorrow. I don't have to decide now. Today.'

Jack inclined his head, as if satisfied, and she felt an immediate qualm. If he thought that *he'd* played any part in the postponement of her wedding day...if he had the crazy idea that she was weakening towards *him*...

And it *was* crazy, she thought wildly. She would never hurt her family by getting involved with the man who'd cruelly rejected her sister and caused them all such pain. Not even if she was tempted...

I'm not! The silent, desperate cry rose from deep within her.

'I'd better go and see Mum,' she gasped, and stumbled away from him, clinging frantically to the thought that Brendan would be back tomorrow and normality would return again, and this madness would be forgotten.

She wished now that she'd rung Brendan, or left a message for him to ring her. But she hadn't wanted to force him into having to make a decision—to stay at his stamp fair or to ditch it and come home. Besides, Brendan would understand that she needed to be alone with her parents at this highly emotional, delicate time.

Brendan always understood.

She and her father took turns at her mother's bedside for the rest of the day, both staying with her until well into the evening. Being a Sunday, her father had no schedules to rearrange, and he'd already cancelled any surgical commitments for the following week—an unheard of occurrence in Kate's experience.

Her mother slept for most of the day, but when awake seemed pleased to see them there.

Jack popped into ICU several times during that quiet

Sunday, which surprised Kate, since there was no deterioration in her mother's condition and the staff were more than capable of watching over her, and could have contacted him if necessary. Why *was* he being so attentive, she found herself wondering, when he must have many other demands on his time, or could have taken a day off?

Was he giving her mother extra care because of Charlotte...because he felt some guilt after all, and wanted for recompense?

She shook her head, rejecting the unlikely notion with a sigh. Jack had made it clear that he felt no guilt, and if he accepted none, why would he feel the need for recompense?

It was more likely that he simply wanted to make sure nothing went wrong in her mother's case so that the Warren-Smith family would have no cause to blame him a second time.

But even that didn't seem to fit the Jack she'd come to know. Her teeth tugged at her lip. Did he feel a special obligation to her mother because she was really Magnus Barratt's patient...and the wife of the country's top cardiac surgeon, Chester Warren-Smith?

As well as the mother of a fellow doctor?

A fellow doctor...he'd come to care about?

Kate swallowed and closed her eyes. She had to stop thinking about him! Jack was simply her mother's neurosurgeon, and nothing else mattered—his feelings, motivations, nothing. What had happened in the past—with Charlotte, with herself five years ago—was behind them now and best forgotten. And the best way to put it out of her mind was to look on Jack purely as a doctor, a professional doing his job.

Brendan was the one she ought to be thinking about. Her future—her future happiness—lay with him.

A deep, tremulous sigh filled her lungs, then whooshed out on a groan.

She rang Brendan from the ER tearoom on Monday morning, during her coffee break. He was already at work, having arrived back in Sydney on the earliest morning flight. She cut off his enthusiastic account of his weekend to tell him about her mother. He was shocked.

'She's coming along well,' she was quick to assure him, thankful that her mother's condition had improved further overnight. 'Though she's not up to having visitors yet, outside the family. She sleeps a fair bit, so Dad or I just sit with her. We simply want her to know we're there.'

'Yes...of course.' Brendan was sympathetic. 'What about the wedding?' he asked, and she stifled a faint twinge. Not, *I should have been there with you*, or *Why didn't you call me immediately? I'd have come straight home*. Not even, *Can I see her?*

The wayward thought occurred to her that if Brendan had been Jack, he'd have considered himself family already, not a visitor, and would have come rushing straight to her mother's bedside—or to *her* side, whether she was at work or not.

Damn Jack, she brooded. He was spoiling everything. He was making her picky and over-critical. None of these things would have bothered her before he turned up.

'I—I think we should postpone the wedding, Brendan,' she said shakily. 'But let's talk about it when

I see you,' she rushed on, when there was a heavy silence the other end.

'Right.' His voice sounded flat. Well, of course he'd be disappointed, she thought, gulping. He'd been so looking forward to their wedding day, and to their honeymoon in Hawaii. But Hawaii would still be there in a few months' time. He'd understand.

'Could we meet at lunchtime?' he asked, sounding anxious now.

'I…promised to spend my lunch break with Mum, to give Dad a breather. How about after dinner tonight, at my place? I want to spend some more time with Mum after I come off duty at five, so that Dad can leave the hospital—he'll have been here all day. I'll have dinner with Mum, then come home after she's settled down for the night. I'll be home by nine-thirty, hopefully.'

'But I thought you and Melanie and I had planned to have dinner together tonight? We planned it last week, before I left.'

Kate felt a stir of irritation. Why did Brendan always find it so hard to adapt? Didn't her understand that things had changed? 'You and Mel can still have dinner together, darling…I'll give her a ring. You can tell *her* all about your weekend. You know how keen she is on stamps.'

When Brendan made no objection to that, she added with forced brightness, 'Let's meet back at our place afterwards…the three of us. To plan what to do about postponing the wedding. We'll have to let everyone know…and cancel the church and the reception and everything.'

She'd half hoped that Brendan might offer to take charge of all that and do it for her, but it was a vain hope.

'OK, I'll see you after dinner, Kate. At your place. Nine-thirty. Mel and I won't be late…we'll make it an early dinner.' Brendan always like to make arrangements perfectly clear. 'Give your mother my love,' he said belatedly, and her heart softened.

He did care. He'd just been a bit dazed and disappointed at the idea of putting off the wedding. It must have come as a blow to him. It would to any man, so close to his wedding day.

'I can see your point about postponing the wedding, Kate,' Brendan conceded when the three of them met later that evening. 'It's the trip to Hawaii that's bothering me. It's all booked and paid for, and I've already let all my clients know that I'll be away for those two weeks.'

Kate stared at him helplessly, with a touch of impatience. People postponed flights and hotel bookings all the time…surely it wasn't so difficult? As for his two weeks off…

'Why don't you still take your fortnight off? I'm still taking mine,' she told him. 'Mum should be out of hospital by then, and she'll need someone to look after her. Dad's not the domestic carer type—and anyway, he has his surgery.'

She looked appealingly at Brendan. If he had time off too, he could spend some of his time with her family…spend his free evenings with *her*. They could take dips in the pool together, or have picnics in the garden with her mother, if she felt up to it. They hadn't spent enough relaxing time together since their engagement.

Brendan couldn't meet her in the eye. There was obviously something else on his mind. 'It's not just the bookings,' he finally admitted, with obvious difficulty. It came out in a rush. 'There's an international stamp fair on in Hawaii during the fortnight we'd planned to be there...'

He trailed off as her eyes widened. 'So that's why you chose to go to Hawaii!' she burst out. Not because of *her*...because he'd wanted to pamper *her*...but because of a stamp fair he'd planned to attend!

'No...not just because of that,' he blustered. 'I knew you'd like Hawaii—you love the beach and the sun. And the stamp fair will only be on for a few days...you wouldn't even have missed me!'

No, she thought caustically. I probably wouldn't. Doesn't every bridegroom want to leave his bride during their honeymoon to go mooning over stamps?

But she was being unfair, she realised in the next breath. What were a few days or hours out of two weeks? She would have been perfectly happy lying on the beach or swimming while Brendan ducked off to look at stamps. He couldn't take as much sun as she could, and he hated the beach. It would have been an ideal holiday for both of them.

'I just wish you'd told me,' she growled. Jack would have been more up front, she thought peevishly—and thinking of Jack only upset her more. What did Jack Savage have to do with her honeymoon? Or with anything!

'Look,' she said, wanting to make amends for thinking about another man—which was far worse than Brendan's minor subterfuge. 'Why don't you still go to Hawaii, darling...at least for the week the stamp fair's on? We'll go somewhere else for our honeymoon...when we decide on a date. There are plenty of other places.'

Brendan eyed her gratefully, his grey eyes more alive now. 'You mean it? I *would* like to go,' he confessed.

'Maybe I can find another stamp collector who'll agree to go with me, to make use of the spare air ticket.'

He glanced at Melanie, who'd been watching and listening in her usual quiet way, without commenting. '*You're* always saying you'd like to go to a stamp fair, Mel,' Brendan reminded her, and looked as surprised as Melanie at what he'd just said. But he pressed on valiantly. 'And you were planning to take a couple of weeks off after the wedding yourself, you said.'

'Oh, yes, but—' Melanie looked flustered, her pale cheeks glowing in a way Kate had seldom seen. '*I* couldn't go with you.' *What would people say?* her big dark eyes seemed to be asking.

'Why not?' Kate heard herself piping up. 'You could do with a holiday, Mel, and you *have* often said that you'd like to go to a stamp fair one day. *And* go overseas. Here's your chance to do both—and the flight and accommodation are already paid for. Brendan could easily change the honeymoon suite to two smaller rooms...'

'Oh, but I couldn't accept—'

'Yes, you could,' Kate insisted, her enthusiasm surprising herself as much as it appeared to be surprising them. 'It can be your bridesmaid's present...from both of us.'

Melanie fingered her throat. 'You—you're already giving me that portrait,' she reminded Kate.

Kate laughed—a trifle unsteadily. 'That was really just practice for me, Mel. You were kind enough to sit for me when I needed a subject to practise on. I'd really like you to go to Hawaii with Brendan, Mel. I mean it. You'd love Hawaii. And you both get on so well...'

What was she doing? she wondered wildly. Trying to push them together?

Was she? They'd always been close, had always stuck

up for each other, and they probably had more in common, she reflected giddily, than she and Brendan did.

Did she secretly *want* them to get together? She felt her breath clogging her throat. Did she hope, deep down, that once they were thrown together—alone together—they would realise they wanted to *stay* together?

If they did, would she feel hurt? Or relieved?

Or simply more confused than ever?

'We'd better make a list of all the people we have to notify,' she said in a rush, changing the subject. 'The guests...the church...the reception centre...the flowers...' She paused, groaning. 'So many calls to make...'

'Don't you worry, Kate... Mel and I will see to it,' Brendan said stoutly, and she looked at him in amazement. Brendan, actually taking over? He was looking far happier too, she noted, not pausing to wonder if it was the stamp fair in Hawaii or his possible new travelling companion who'd put that light in his eye.

'You will?' she asked, her voice unsteady.

'Of course we will,' Melanie put in, her gentle voice unusually animated, her dark eyes flashing with purpose. 'That's what bridesmaids are for...to take the worry and pressure off the bride.'

Kate felt her cheeks glowing hot. Could Melanie tell that she was under pressure? That she was confused and uncertain? She swallowed hard. Dear Mel saw too much at times. She'd often asked her if she really loved Brendan, she recalled now, and shown concern when she'd admitted to pre-wedding jitters.

Mel cares more about Brendan than I do, she thought suddenly. Wonderingly.

And maybe, in Hawaii, Brendan would realise that he was starting to care for Melanie...

If he did, what would he decide to do about it?

'I think it's time I went to bed,' she mumbled, jumping up. 'Would you mind awfully?' she asked them. 'I'm really so tired...it's been a harrowing couple of days. I haven't slept much for the past two nights.'

'Of course you must get your sleep.' Brendan was already on his feet. 'We'll do what needs to be done, love...even if it takes all night.'

This was Brendan talking? The man who hated staying up late? Who never took charge?

'Goodnight, darling.' He bent to kiss her goodnight.

She strained towards him, catching his kiss on her lips...hoping he would let his lips linger a moment...applying pressure with her own to show him that she was more than eager to comply. But he drew back almost as soon as their lips touched, leaving her with a sense of dissatisfaction...and vague disappointment.

Of course, Brendan would never kiss her passionately in front of Melanie—or anyone else. In fact, he was careful not to kiss her too passionately even when they were alone, as if worried his feelings might flare out of control. And he'd sworn not to let that happen until their wedding night.

Well, now he'd have to wait a few months longer, until they set another date. How did he feel about that? she wondered curiously, with a strange sense of detachment, as she left them and went up to her room.

How did she feel about it herself, for that matter?

She felt nothing. Just numb.

She was too tired to feel. That was all it was.

CHAPTER ELEVEN

IT WAS a relief, knowing that the pressure of the wedding was off. Kate was able to concentrate on her mother, on her work at the hospital, and spend time with her father. She'd seen more of him in this past week than she'd seen in the past six months. She relished the new closeness between them. It even encouraged her to broach the subject of Jack Savage one evening, when she came into her mother's room after work to relieve her father, who'd been there for most of the day.

Her mother was dozing at the time, and Kate felt confident that her father wouldn't risk waking her, or upsetting her, by losing his temper.

'Dad...' she ventured. 'Now that Jack—Dr Savage—has shown that he's a—a caring, responsible person—surgeon—and not the callous monster we all thought him...don't you think we could—?'

'Forget it. I'll never forgive him for what he did to my daughter,' her father rumbled over her, though he spoke with a hoarse weariness rather than the bitter hatred of the past. 'He may be a fine neurosurgeon—and I'm grateful to him for what he's done for your mother—but that's where it ends. Don't ask any more from me.'

Kate drew in a deep quivering breath. 'Dad, I don't think Jack realised how deeply Charlotte felt about him. When he left her—left Australia—he had no idea she—she would go to pieces the way she did. He didn't hurt her deliberately. He didn't even know that he had.'

She rushed on before her father could cut her off.

'You can't blame him for wanting to go overseas to train, or wanting to work with the top neurosurgeons in America.' She raised appealing eyes to her father. 'Dad, it happened seven years ago. Charlotte was ambitious herself,' she reminded him. 'Losing out on that surgical registrar job really upset her. It was that as much as losing Jack…Jonathan Savage…'

Her father raised a weary hand, as if to close the matter. But at least he'd listened to her, she thought with a sigh. That was something. They'd never even been able to talk about it before.

'And people do change,' said a quiet voice from the bed. 'Jack Savage is a different man now, Chester…a very warm, understanding and compassionate man. As well as a man of integrity and a brilliant expert in his field.'

Kate's eyes widened. Her mother must have been listening all along! Hearing her mother speaking up in defence of Jack Savage—and so glowingly—gave her a strange fluttery feeling inside…though she didn't want to delve too closely into the reason for it.

'Well, I'll leave you with Kate, dear.' Her father leaned down to kiss his wife, then ambled out with a farewell smile for Kate, who pulled a chair up and sat down. As usual she'd brought some work with her—on this occasion some medical histories to write up. Some evenings she brought a medical textbook, or a pile of medical journals from the hospital library. It made her mother feel better about her busy daughter 'wasting her evenings,' as she put it, 'with her ailing mother.'

Since she'd been back on day shift Kate had fallen into a routine, working in the ER during the day and spending her evenings with her mother. Edith was now in a private single-bed room, and allowed to have visitors, though her husband still kept them to a minimum.

Both Brendan and Melanie had been in a couple of times, but neither had stayed long, not wanting to tire Edith or get in the way.

Kate, though she tried not to, couldn't help noticing the difference between Brendan's visits and Jack's. Brendan almost sidled in, taking up a position at a discreet distance from the bed, looking stiff and uncomfortable. Edith's bandages were now off, and her shaven head, with a long scar and staples clearly visible, seemed to embarrass him. He hardly knew where to look. He spoke in a low, grave voice, as if afraid that Edith would disintegrate before his eyes if he raised it, or said the wrong thing.

Jack always strode in smiling, with a joke or a quip on his lips, and her mother always brightened noticeably at the sight of him.

Kate hadn't realised that her own eyes lit up too, until her mother commented on it.

'You like Jack Savage, don't you, dear? And I've a feeling he likes you,' she said, startling Kate. 'He's taken to popping in to see me at night, I've noticed, when *you're* here—even though he's already been to see me during the day. And I've seen the way he looks at you…'

'Mum! Don't be ridiculous!' Kate felt her heart racing, her face heating. 'He knows I'm engaged to be married.'

'But he'll hear soon enough that you've put off your wedding, dear. It's all around the hospital already. And he's bound to wonder if you've just postponed it…or cancelled it altogether.'

Kate stared at her mother. 'But we've just—just—'

She gulped. Was her mother wondering too? 'I want *you* at my wedding, Mum. That's the only reason I—'

'Is it, love?' her mother broke in gently. 'You must be very sure, darling...and I don't think you are. Not any more.'

Kate opened her mouth, and then shut it again, painfully plucking her gaze from her mother's. For someone recovering from brain surgery, her mother was amazingly perceptive. How could she have guessed? She *wasn't* sure any more. Maybe she never had been.

'Wh-what makes you think that?' she stalled.

Her mother reached for her hand. 'I've sensed it for some time, dear. You and Brendan are more like—well, like good friends rather than a couple in love. The spark that should be there...the glow...well, it's simply not there.'

'Mum, I've been worried about *you*...'

'Yes, I know that, dear, but I *have* seen a spark in your eyes...when Jack Savage comes into the room.'

Panicked eyes flew to her mother's. 'There's nothing between Jack Savage and me!' She flushed at her own vehemence. 'There n-never could be!'

Her mother pursed her lips, her eyes pensive now. 'Maybe we've been too harsh on him...where Charlotte's concerned. I mean, it's not as if your sister was engaged to him...or even living with him. They just worked together...and had an affair.'

Kate's heart flared with a crazy hope, then died. Her father still hadn't forgiven Jack and never would. It would be unbearably cruel to *him* for her to get entangled with Jack. And Jack, she was certain, would never want anything to do with *him*...with Charlotte's family.

'Mum, you don't have to worry...there's nothing between Jack and me,' she repeated heavily. She drew in a tremulous breath. 'Just because Brendan and I...because I'm not sure any more...doesn't mean...' She gulped back a rising sob and clamped her mouth shut, afraid that if she went on she might break down and burst into tears.

'Darling, if you don't love Brendan, wouldn't it be fairer to tell him now, to be honest with him, rather than keep him dangling for months longer? I know you don't want to hurt him, dear, but it will hurt him more if you postpone the wedding to another date...and *then* decide that you should have cancelled it altogether.'

Kate gaped at her mother. It was almost as if she were urging her...as if she would *condone*... 'Mum, I... I...' She glanced up in relief as an old friend of her mother's poked her head round the door. 'Come in, Barbara!' She leapt up thankfully to let her mother's visitor take her place at Edith's bedside. 'I was just going down to grab something to eat.'

She excused herself and slipped away, leaving the two alone.

She had a lot to think about.

It was after nine-thirty when she finally left the hospital. When she reached the car park she heard footsteps behind her, gaining rapidly. Since it was after visiting hours, and the car park was deserted just now, she flicked a wary glance behind, almost missing her footing when she recognised the tall, broad-shouldered frame of Jack Savage closing the gap between them.

'Oh...hullo, Jack,' she said weakly as he caught up. 'What are you doing here at the hospital on a Saturday night?' She asked the question flippantly, more for something to say than out of any burning interest. Or so she told herself.

'Waiting for you.'

She missed another step. 'Me? Why?' She felt a prickling sensation down her arms. She'd been trying to keep out of his way all week, as much as possible, not wanting him to think she'd put off her wedding because of him. She'd only seen him at close range when he'd popped in to see her mother at night—and she'd kept any conversation short and impersonal, sometimes slipping out of the room altogether until he'd gone.

'I hear you've cancelled your wedding.'

Her throat constricted. 'Postponed it,' she corrected, even though it wasn't quite the truth—or it wouldn't be after tomorrow. She'd rung Brendan while Barbara was with her mother, to ask if they could meet in the morning—Sunday being her day off. She hadn't told him why, and Brendan hadn't asked. He'd just said, yes, they both needed to talk. To set a new date for the wedding, she assumed he'd meant.

The thought of hurting him weighed heavily, but she couldn't let things go on any longer now that her mother had forced her to face up to the truth.

She couldn't marry Brendan.

She didn't love him.

And now that she'd acknowledged it, even if only to herself as yet, she could hardly go on promising to spend the rest of her life with him. She'd believed—*made* herself believe—that the fondness she felt for Brendan *was* love, or would be enough, and maybe it would have been if Jack hadn't come back into her life. Jack had made her realise, reluctantly and devastatingly, what real love was—pain, passion, shared laughter, an all-consuming need—and that anything less would be impossible, unfair to both Brendan and herself.

But could anything ever come of her love for Jack?

Charlotte's ghost, even after seven years, was still a very real presence. Her father would never accept Jack Savage into the Warren-Smith fold. It would hurt him too much. And she—caught in the middle—would have to make a choice. If she chose Jack, she would have to turn her back on her father, which would hurt him even more. She couldn't do that to him. He'd already lost one daughter.

Anyway, with the lingering antagonism between Jack and her father, Jack was unlikely to *want* to be a part of her family, even if he felt something for her...something more than a physical need.

She sighed. Even if he did care for her, he'd told her that marriage wasn't a priority, and to her love and marriage went hand in hand. An affair—even living together—would never be enough for her.

But if *she* could change her mind about never wanting to marry a doctor, maybe Jack would change his mind about marriage...

'Your mother seems to think your wedding will never take place,' Jack said from behind, his voice splintering her thoughts.

Her head snapped round, shock in her eyes. 'You've been discussing me with my mother?' Just what had her mother told him?

His teeth gleamed in the diffused lamplight. 'Your mother and I enjoy our little chats when I come to see her during the day.'

'And my father too?' She raked him with her eyes. 'He's been with my mother every day this week. Has he joined in your little chats?' *That* she would find hard to believe. Especially if she was the subject!

'Your father normally leaves the room when I come in,' Jack said dryly. 'He leaves me to examine my patient in private.' He paused, then asked, 'Are you telling me your mother has it wrong? Is your wedding going ahead or not? Now that I've met your fiancé, I can see why your mother feels unsure about him being the right man for you, Kate. He doesn't seem your type at all.'

Her heart lurched. She was tempted to ask who he thought *was* her type, but she thought of Brendan, and said instead, 'Oh, you can tell that, can you, after a single passing glimpse?' She recalled Jack striding into her mother's room one night, just as Brendan was backing out. How had he summed up her fiancé so quickly?

'I know who *is* your type,' Jack said roughly, his great shadow blocking out much of the lamplight as they paused at her car.

She began to tremble, every nerve-end tingling at his closeness. She didn't trust herself to speak.

'And you know it too,' Jack murmured. 'Even though others mightn't agree.'

Her breath fluttered in her throat, the resigned cynicism in his voice tearing at her heart. 'Others' meaning her father, of course.

'Jack...please...' She looked up at him helplessly. She mustn't listen. She was still wearing Brendan's ring. 'My mother should never have said what she did.' Why *had* she?

'Your mother only wants what's best for you, Kate. As I do.'

He touched her arm as he said it, and flames leapt along her skin, her self-control slipping. She raised a trembling chin, fighting an overwhelming urge to lean into him, to melt into his arms. But she mustn't. She couldn't.

With difficulty, she assumed a teasing note. 'Is this the concerned doctor talking? Or the concerned colleague?' She groaned inwardly as the huskiness in her voice betrayed her.

His fingers closed round her arms, forcing her closer. 'You know it's more than that, Kate. And if you're intending to break off your engagement—'

'Jack, no! Stop!' She felt a flash of panic. 'Let me go! *Please,*' she begged. She couldn't think straight when he was holding her so close. 'I'm not breaking it off because of you,' she told him shakily. 'I'm breaking it off because—because I've realised I'm not in love with Brendan and it's not fair to—to—'

Jack's lips stopped her. As their warmth seeped into hers, her will-power dissolved, her mouth melting under his. For a few wild, glorious seconds she let her senses take control, let her heart rule her head, her blood throbbing in her ears as her body overheated, the way it always did with Jack.

She slid her arms round his neck, her body straining into his, her breath rasping in her throat as her fevered lips sucked and clung to his. It was Jack who drew back first, with a soft laugh.

'Now tell me I mean nothing to you!' Triumph glittered in his eyes.

She looked up at him helplessly. 'Jack, it's not that... I don't want... *Please* Jack, let me go!' she begged as his fingers tightened on her arms. 'We mustn't!' It was a hoarse cry. If anyone saw her kissing Jack Savage the night before she broke up with her fiancé...

She shivered. If her father heard about it, he'd blame Jack for coming between them and would hate him even more. She couldn't let that happen.

'I'm still engaged to Brendan!' she reminded him.

'But not for much longer...if you're honest with yourself, Kate. And honest with him. And, dammit, honest with me.' His voice had roughened again. 'No matter what obstacles lie ahead of us, Kate, I'm not going to lose you again.'

Her head spun. Again? He had to be talking about five years ago. Losing her...because of Charlotte.

He didn't intend to let Charlotte come between them again!

She gazed up at him, resisting the urge to stroke his dark hair back from his brow, resisting the urge to blurt out how she felt about him, how she'd always felt about him.

'I—I'm seeing Brendan in the morning,' she admitted huskily. 'And I—I'll need some time to myself, Jack...after that.'

She didn't want her father accusing Jack of breaking up her engagement...he had enough ammunition to throw at Jack already. Neither did she want her father, or anyone else, to think that she'd turned to Jack Savage on the rebound. Or for Jack himself to think it.

She saw a tenderness in his eyes that she'd never seen before. As if he understood. As if he...as if he...

Emotion swelled in her throat. She held his gaze a brief second longer, showing her own feelings as plainly as he was. Then she swung away from him and made a dive for her car.

'Goodnight, Jack!'

'Goodnight, my golden mermaid.' The same tenderness was in his voice, and, hearing it, she felt her heart soar, pierced with an exquisite longing. 'Until I can hold you in my arms again,' she heard him call after her.

As she started up her car with fumbling fingers, she felt a tingly shiver down her spine, part ecstasy, part fear.

Would it ever happen? Did Jack really feel the same way she felt? Would they ever have a future together...the kind of future she longed for?

It seemed too beautiful a dream to come true.

CHAPTER TWELVE

THE sunny spring day that was to have been her wedding day came and went—the day after her mother came home from the hospital. Brendan flew off to Hawaii the following morning, and Melanie went with him.

Brendan had accepted the break-up of their engagement with a dignity and calmness that had relieved and surprised Kate. It was almost as if he'd been having similar feelings to her own...as if he agreed that the close affection they'd always felt for each other was no longer enough.

When she'd told Melanie that Brendan was now a free man, that there was nothing to stop her travelling to Hawaii with him if she wished, and that Brendan still wanted her to go, Melanie had blushed revealingly, causing Kate to wonder how she'd never seen it before. Melanie was in love with Brendan!

And if she knew Brendan—Kate crossed her fingers hopefully—it wouldn't be long before he was in love with Melanie. He was halfway in love with her already, she suspected. They'd always been good friends and they had much in common—interests, ideals and even personalities. Now there was nothing to stop them finding out just how deeply they did feel about each other.

As for herself, she was spending her honeymoon vacation at her family home, helping her father care for her steadily improving mother, while Anna, their housekeeper, kept the household running during the week.

It was both an agony and a relief being away from

173

Jack. At the hospital Kate had been finding it harder and harder to hide her feelings each time Jack strode into the ER, or into her mother's room, or when they shared a lift, or passed each other in the canteen, or in a hospital corridor.

But two weeks away from him altogether, not seeing him at all, seemed an eternity. She wondered if he was missing her as much. Maybe not, she mused wistfully, sudden misgivings threatening her fragile outer calm. Maybe he'd decided there were too many obstacles to their getting together, or that the pain it would cause her father would ultimately affect their own relationship.

By her second weekend at home she was a bundle of nerves, though she tried her best to hide it from her mother, and from her father when he was at home.

It was on the following Tuesday that the routine she'd fallen into came to a shattering halt.

She'd popped out to have lunch at a nearby restaurant with Georgia, who had a couple of hours free. Her father was at home with her mother, having taken the day off in readiness for a visit during the afternoon by Kate's aunt, Sarah, his wife's sister.

When Kate came home later in the afternoon she found her father slumped in an armchair with his head in his hands. He glanced up as she walked into the room, and she cried out at his sickly pallor and the deep lines etched in his face.

'Dad, what's wrong?' She ran to him. 'Is it Mum? Where is she?'

'She's upstairs with your aunt Sarah.' He shook his head, his voice the thin croak of a defeated old man. 'No, it's not your mother. It's this…' He waved a hand, and for the first time Kate noticed the papers scattered around his chair, and what looked like a leather-bound diary on his lap.

And an old leather briefcase, lying open at his feet, with more papers visible inside. A stained leather strap lay beside it.

Her eyes widened. It couldn't be...

She snapped her gaze back to her father's face.

'It's your sister's briefcase—the one I gave her when she graduated,' he dragged out. 'The police found it in a derelict building up in Queensland, of all places, where it must have been dumped years ago. Someone had forced it open—thieves presumably—then abandoned it. Though how on earth it got to Queensland...'

'It must be the briefcase that Charlotte asked her friend Diana to look after for her,' Kate forced out. 'Diana was going to hand it over to me a—a few years ago, but it was stolen from her beach-house up on the Sunshine Coast before she could. It's been missing ever since. How come the police sent it to—to you, Dad?'

Her father heaved a sigh. 'It had "Dr C. Warren-Smith" engraved on it, and they thought it belonged to me.' His mouth twisted. 'Apparently my name is well-known, even up in Queensland. They sent it down to the police in Sydney, who brought it here to me.'

He shook his head in pained disbelief. 'I just can't believe she could have done what she did. My beautiful, talented daughter. To feel she had to do such a thing. I can't think what possessed her to do it. She had the whole world in front of her.'

Kate felt prickles along her spine. 'You...you're talking about her overdose?' Her eyes flickered to his lap. 'Is—is that her diary?'

'Yes, it's her diary.' Her father almost spat the word, his eyes showing a different kind of pain than in the past. A demoralised, grimly bitter pain. 'But I wasn't talking about her overdose.'

He flung the diary to the floor as if it were something foul and rotten. 'I was wrong about Jonathan Savage. Totally wrong. All these years…and he said nothing in his own defence…nothing against Charlotte…he kept the sick truth to himself. He was *protecting* me… protecting my daughter's memory…protecting us all from the shame…the humiliation…'

'Dad!' Shocked, Kate dropped to her knees beside his chair, clutching her father's arm. 'What are you saying?' She couldn't believe her ears. Her father had been wrong about Jack? Jack had been protecting them?

'What shame?' she breathed. 'What humiliation?'

She felt her father shudder under her fingers. 'Remember that scientific paper your sister published…for the work she'd been doing on surgical hypothermia? It was Jonathan Savage's work…his research…his findings. She was only assisting him. Yet she went ahead and wrote and published that paper under her own name, claiming the work solely as her own, without even acknowledging Savage!'

'Oh, Dad,' Kate turned stunned eyes to his. 'Are you—are you sure?'

He let out a harsh laugh. 'It's all here…in her diary. And these…' He pointed to the papers scattered about. 'These are some of their work papers…showing—*proving*—that it was essentially Savage's research!'

'But why would she do such a thing?' Kate whispered, hating to see her father's distress. 'She was so talented, so clever. She didn't need to—'

'It seems she wasn't as talented or as clever as she made out.' The bitter edge to his voice pierced Kate's heart. 'Ambitious, yes. Blazingly ambitious. She was determined to do well…for *my* sake.' A muscle twitched at his jaw. '*I* pushed her into achieving more and more…striving for more than she was capable of. My expectations were too high. And she didn't want to disappoint me.'

Kate tried to speak, but he rasped over her, 'She thought the kudos from that research paper would help her to win the surgical registrar job she wanted so badly. But she didn't impress at the interview.' He shook his head. 'I put it down to nerves…a bad day…but the truth was, she simply wasn't good enough.'

'Dad, you mustn't blame yourself.' Kate's sympathy washed over him. 'Charlotte was determined and capable enough to have achieved all her ambitions eventually, and she would have made a fine surgeon…if she'd been prepared to be patient and to put in the hard work. She made one bad, reckless mistake.'

Her mind was already flitting to Jack. He'd known what Charlotte had done seven years ago, but he'd never told a soul, never revealed the truth, not even when she—Charlotte's sister—had met him two years later at Shelly Beach and reviled him for what he'd done to her sister…not even when he'd come back to Sydney five years after that, to find her family still blaming him for Charlotte's death.

Suddenly everything became painfully clear to her. Jack's harsh attitude towards Charlotte, his coldness towards her father, his initial mistrust of *her*, after he'd found out who she was. He must have thought, until just recently, that all the Warren-Smiths were tarred with the same brush…as ruthlessly ambitious and as lacking in moral integrity as Charlotte!

Poor Charlotte, she thought, with a rush of sympathy for her tragic sister. The guilt of what she'd done must have eaten away at her…the shame, the sense of failure, the bitter realisation that she would never be the dazzling star her father believed her to be…that she'd built herself up to be. And she'd lost the man she loved at the same time, killing any feeling he'd had for her. Jack must have been sickened by what she'd done and walked out on her in disgust.

'I can't live with the pain,' Charlotte had written in her final note…

Not the pain of losing him, but the pain of what she'd done…the guilt, the regret.

The words *"Johnnie, forgive me"* made more sense now too. Her sister hadn't been referring to her suicide, wanting to relieve Jack of any feeling of blame. She'd been begging forgiveness for the terrible wrong she'd done him.

Tears pricked at Kate's eyes. When she'd told Jack that Charlotte had written the words *'forgive me'* he'd said nothing. He'd kept the shocking truth to himself, still determined to protect her and her family, no matter how it reflected on him.

She buried her own pain to attend to her father's.

'Dad,' she said gently. 'If Charlotte had had no conscience or regrets, she would have destroyed all these papers…and destroyed her diary…the evidence…not left them for her family to read. Well, left them for me,' she admitted. 'She wanted to spare *you*, Dad.'

She bit her lip. 'Charlotte told Diana that if anything happened to her, to hold onto the briefcase for a while and then give it to me…that I'd know what to do with it.'

'And would you have kept it from me?' her father asked, lifting heavy eyes. 'Sparing me the hurt…the shame...the bitter realisation that my daughter was a cheat and a fraud?'

'Oh, Dad, I wouldn't have wanted to hurt you any more than Charlotte did,' Kate cried. 'But I think my sister would have wanted me to let Jack Savage know that she'd left a diary and documents behind, admitting what she'd done and taking the blame for everything that had happened. It might have softened his attitude towards her...knowing that she was sorry for the wrong she'd done him and had left behind proof that he could use if he wanted to.'

She caught her father's arm. 'Dad, he's not likely to expose her now, if he didn't do it seven years ago. Though it's a wonder he didn't tell *somebody*—when she first published the article, I mean—knowing the research was his.'

'Charlotte begged him not to,' her father ground out. 'She told him that with his brilliance he would get to the top regardless, whereas she would have to claw her way up, and needed all the help she could get. She said that if he really cared about her, he would say nothing and let her take the credit.'

'And he didn't say anything,' Kate murmured, unaware of the yearning in her voice, in her eyes. 'He must have loved her very much.' Loved and hated her in equal measure, perhaps.

Would he ever come to love her as much? She sighed. After what her family had done to him, and the vitriol she'd poured on him herself in the past, she was surprised that he could feel anything for her at all! Perhaps he was already coming to the same conclusion.

'Loved her?' Her father shook his head. 'Whatever he felt for her, it wasn't love. If he'd loved her, he would have forgiven her anything...even a thing like that...and stayed to protect her...cover for her.'

The way her father, Kate wondered pityingly, would be trying to understand and forgive what his daughter had done?

'He told her he had nothing but contempt for her,' Chester wrenched out, 'and didn't want anything more to do with her. That's why he went off to America so abruptly. To get away from her. And I can't say I blame him!'

'Dad, Jack's not bitter about Charlotte or our family any more,' Kate shakily assured him. 'Look at all he's done for us...for Mum...how wonderful he's been to her, and the time he's spent with her. And he—he's been equally k-kind to me.' A trembling sigh slipped from her lips.

Her father gave her a brief, probing look, before hauling himself from his chair. 'I'm going to see him. Now. To apologise for the grave injustice we've done him.' His face was tight, his jaw set, his anguished eyes tearing at Kate's heart.

'Dad, wait!' She sprang to her feet. 'Do you want me to come with you? Or can I speak to him for you? I—I'll tell him you're too upset. He'll understand.'

'No.' A firm, unequivocal *no*. 'I have to do this myself. And my colleagues will be hearing about it too.'

'Oh, Dad, I'm sure Jack won't want—'

'Tell your mother I've gone out, will you? Just say something's come up. I'll explain to her later...when your aunt's gone.' He paused a moment. 'Why don't you take a swim before dinner, Kate, while your aunt's with your mother? It'll relax you.'

Kate turned to him with a misty smile. Even in his despair, he was able to spare a thought for her. How he's changed, she thought, from the man—the cold distant figure—he used to be.

'I think I will.' She needed something to relax her, and take her mind off Jack and the day's shocking revelations. Would Jack forgive her father for maligning him all these years? Would he forgive *her*?

She did a third leisurely lap of the pool. The cool water flowing through her curls and along her body was soothing...relaxing...washing away her tension. Her head felt clear again. She was even daring to hope...to dream...just a little.

When she reached the deep end of the pool she paused for breath, squeezing her eyes and blinking a few times to clear them. She lifted a hand to push her streaming hair back from her face. As she glanced up she saw a pair of bare legs. Tanned, powerful legs. Her bemused gaze travelled higher.

A breathtaking vision unfolded. A glorious, splendidly built vision in brief copper-coloured swim-trunks. A massive-shouldered, superbly muscled, lightly bronzed Samson, with soft black hair and piercing blue eyes.

She blinked. She had to be hallucinating. Her mind had conjured an incredible dream. She was back at Shelly Beach, her gaze drinking in the most magnificent sight she had ever seen. Only her sketchbook was missing.

The vision smiled, the beguiling lips stretching, slashing the strong face with very real lines. And a very real, very familiar voice rumbled into the balmy afternoon air.

'Is my golden mermaid ready to be rescued?'

Her heart soared. 'Oh, Jack!' she squeaked. 'How can *you* be here? How did you know I'd be here in the pool?'

Her *father* must have sent him! A miracle in itself. She glanced round, but there was no sign of Chester.

Jack took a step forward, before diving neatly into the water. Grace and lithe power in motion. He bobbed up beside her, water glistening on his face, pouring from his hair, sharpening the blue of his eyes.

'Your father said you'd invited me over for a swim.' His eyes scorched over her face, her eyes, her lips. 'There were no pressing demands at the hospital, so I gave myself the rest of the afternoon off.' He slid a big, long-fingered hand round her neck, under the wet tangle of her hair, kicking his legs to stay afloat.

'Oh, Jack,' she breathed. 'We're so sorry about—'

'Hush.' He touched a wet finger to her lips. 'It's all behind us now. We can finally look ahead, Kate…with no ghosts or shadows between us. From now on it's only the present and the future that matter. Your future, Kate…and mine.'

She gazed up at him, amazed at what she was hearing. She was in a daze, her heart flying like a bird, delicious quivery tingles tumbling down her spine. The way he was looking at her…the way he was smiling.

She swallowed, afraid her heart would burst with happiness.

'Is—is my father all right?' she asked in a hoarse whisper. 'It really hit him hard, Jack. Charlotte was his favourite…his shining star…'

'You're his shining star now, Kate,' Jack said gently, his fingers tangling in her damp curls, his free hand gripping the edge of the pool to support them both. 'And it's because of the person you are…nothing to do with achievement or ambition, even though you've already proved yourself a fine doctor…and a promising artist…'

His eyes glinted wickedly. 'One day I might even let

you sketch me in the nude again...on condition the artist is similarly disrobed. Though I'd much rather we did something else under those conditions.'

Her cheeks glowed pink, her heartbeat mingling with his as his muscled chest came into contact with her bikini-clad breasts. She flicked another glance around. 'Dad followed you back here?'

Jack's lips brushed over her damp brow. 'He wanted to go to his own hospital for a while, but first I extracted his promise not to say anything to anyone but your mother. Charlotte's lapse seven years ago is past history, I told him, and no longer matters to me. Let her memory remain as it is.'

'Oh, Jack, you're incredible. An angel. I don't deserve a—a friend like you.'

'A friend?' His lip quirked. 'I want you to be more than a friend to me, Kate. A lot more.' The glittering blue eyes softened. 'And I have your father's blessing. The last thing he said to me was, "Take care of her, Jack." I'm not sure how I managed to answer, but I assured him I would.'

There was a huskiness in his voice that brought a hot prickle to her eyes and a lump of emotion to her throat. Anyone believing that high-powered specialist surgeons lacked emotion should see Jack now, she thought, swallowing.

As for her father...he *knew*! He knew how she felt about Jack. Had he seen something in her eyes, read something in her defence of Jack, or had her mother said something to him? It hardly mattered. She had his blessing, and the ghosts haunting her family and Jack Savage had been laid to rest for all time.

'I intend to take good care of *you* too,' she assured

Jack hoarsely. 'I can't believe that you...that I...that there's nothing to—'

'You'd better believe it,' Jack growled, his voice thick, his eyes burning into hers with a melting tenderness. 'But enough talk...' With one hand he moulded her to him until their wet bodies were clinging, flesh to flesh, heartbeat to heartbeat. 'I want to do something I've longed to do for five interminably long years.'

His face, his mouth, were wondrously close, his blazing eyes riveted to hers. 'Kiss the woman I love, knowing there's nothing to stop her kissing me back without guilt, without restraint, without anything or anyone between us...and maybe even with the same love I feel for her. You *are* ready now, my golden mermaid?'

Love... She raised a radiant face to his. She was too choked up to speak. But her arm was already winding round his neck. *'The woman I love,'* he'd said. And he was real. He was *here*. And her father, of all people, had sent him to her!

When his mouth captured hers, sheer bliss exploded inside her. This time, as she showed him in no uncertain terms, there was nothing to stop her giving in to the wondrous burning need swirling through her, igniting her body as only he could. She kissed him with all the passion and longing and joy she'd been repressing for far too long.

She couldn't have said afterwards how they managed to get from the pool to Jack's car, and from there to her house in Paddington, but that was where they ended up, and where they sealed their love, gasping out the words *'I love you'* over and over, their longing and their hunger for each other engulfing them, spiralling out of control, hurtling them all the way to paradise.

As they lay back in each other's arms, gloriously

sated, at least for the time being, Kate murmured with a sigh, 'If Brendan finds he loves Melanie the way I love you, Jack, he won't be able to wait either. To think that he and I were prepared to wait until our wedding night! It just proves we weren't really in love, or nothing could have kept us from each other.'

As the words 'wedding night' left her lips, a wave of shyness swept over her. There was a glimmer of uncertainty in her eyes as she glanced up into the face of the man she loved, and always would. Jack had told her once that marriage wasn't a priority. But there had been insurmountable obstacles then...

'Nothing's going to keep us from each other, ever again,' Jack promised her. 'We're going to get married, my love...but we'll give our friends and colleagues some time to get used to the idea of us being together. But not too long... You *will* marry me, won't you, Kate?' Now he was the one who was uncertain. Jack the invincible, looking uncertain!

She nodded, her eyes shining with her love for him. 'I'll elope, if you like. I'd run off with you tomorrow.'

'No.' He kissed the silky hollow of her throat. 'We're not going to sneak away and marry in secret. We're going to do this properly, with all the trimmings and with plenty of notice. So keep your wedding dress, my darling, and be prepared to plan another wedding. We'll announce our engagement when your mother's better...by which time, I have a feeling, Brendan will have announced his engagement to Melanie.'

His eyes danced above hers. 'He'll want to make an honest woman of Mel after running away to Hawaii with her. I wouldn't be surprised if they come back married themselves.'

'Oh, I do hope they do!' Kate snuggled deeper into his arms. 'They'll be perfect for each other.'

He brushed the curls back from her face, and she marvelled again at the lightness of his touch, at how a man so big and so powerful could be so achingly gentle. 'And Melanie can still be your bridesmaid—or matron of honour, if she gets married first.' Jack smiled into her eyes.

'Oh, yes, Jack, that would be wonderful.'

Jack pursed his lips as he considered something else. 'I might even ask Brendan to be my best man...so he can partner Melanie at our wedding. Then everyone will know there are no hard feelings, that you and he simply made a mistake...and discovered the right partners in time.'

'Oh, Jack, it's no wonder I love you.' She slipped her arms round his neck and held him as if she would never let him go.

'And it's no wonder I love you, my entrancing sea nymph...and everyone else loves you too.' He covered her mouth with kisses.

As she came up for air, her eyes drowning in the shimmering blue of his, she asked tentatively, 'Jack, if—if I hadn't broken off my engagement to Brendan, would you have stood by and let me go ahead with the wedding?'

An impish sparkle lit his eyes. 'I was confident you wouldn't go ahead. I could see your defences were crumbling. Your surrender was inevitable.'

'Oh, it was, was it?' At the very word, she felt ready to surrender all over again. 'Well, you're right... Once you came back into my life, I knew I could never marry Brendan. Or anyone else. From now on, you'll always be the number one man in my life. The *only* man.'

'I'd better be. And we'll show your father that you've made the right choice.'

'I'm sure he's happy already, Jack...because he knows that you'll make *me* happy.' She clung to him. 'I love you, Jack. So much!' As she pressed her naked body into the powerful warmth of his an exquisite ache stirred deep inside her, and her back arched in a spasm of desire.

She felt his own body respond with the same urgency, heard him moan, 'I'll never get tired of hearing you say you love me, my golden mermaid...or of saying it to you,' before both of them were caught up in another wave of glorious need, rocketing them to new heights, and ever more rapturous wonders.

It was like a dream. A fairy tale.

A dream that had finally come true.

MILLS & BOON®

Makes any time special

Enjoy a romantic novel from
Mills & Boon®

Presents™ *Enchanted*™ *Temptation*

Historical Romance™ *Medical Romance*™

FREE!

4 Books
and a surprise gift!

We would like to take this opportunity to thank you for reading this Mills & Boon® book by offering you the chance to take FOUR more specially selected titles from the Enchanted™ series absolutely FREE! We're also making this offer to introduce you to the benefits of the Reader Service™—

★ FREE home delivery
★ FREE gifts and competitions
★ FREE monthly Newsletter
★ Books available before they're in the shops
★ Exclusive Reader Service discounts

Accepting these FREE books and gift places you under no obligation to buy; you may cancel at any time, even after receiving your free shipment. Simply complete your details below and return the entire page to the address below. *You don't even need a stamp!*

YES! Please send me 4 free Enchanted books and a surprise gift. I understand that unless you hear from me, I will receive 6 superb new titles every month for just £2.40 each, postage and packing free. I am under no obligation to purchase any books and may cancel my subscription at any time. The free books and gift will be mine to keep in any case.

N9EB

Ms/Mrs/Miss/Mr ....Initials ....
                                                                                                BLOCK CAPITALS PLEASE
Surname ....
Address ....
....
....Postcode ....

Send this whole page to:
THE READER SERVICE, FREEPOST CN81, CROYDON, CR9 3WZ
(Eire readers please send coupon to: P.O. BOX 4546, DUBLIN 24.)

The Drifter

SUSAN WIGGS

"Susan Wiggs turns an able and sensual hand to
the...story of the capable, strait-laced spinster
and sensual roving rogue."
—Publishers Weekly

MIRA® **Available from 19th February 1999**